CATASTROPHE
IN
CASEVILLE

Here's what readers from around the country are saying about Johnathan Rand's AMERICAN CHILLERS:

"Hey! I've read a lot of your boos and I really liked WASH-INGTON WAX MUSEUM. It was the best!"

-Olivia F., age 10, Michigan

"I'm your biggest fan! I read all of your books! Can you write a book and put my name in it?"

-Antonio D.,age 11, Florida

"We drove from Missouri to Michigan just to visit Chillermania!" It's the coolest book store in the world!

-Katelyn H., age 12, Missouri

"Thanks for writing such awesome books! I own every single American Chiller, but I can't decide which one I like best."

-Caleb C., Age 10, New Mexico

"Johnathan Rand is my favorite author in the whole world! Why does he wear those freaky glasses?"

-Sarah G., age 8, Montana

"I read all of your books, but the scariest book was TERRI-FYING TOYS OF TENNESSEE, because I live in Tennessee and I am kind of scared of toys."

-Ana E., age 10, Tennessee

"I've read all of your books, and they're great! I'm reading CURSE OF THE CONNECTICUT COYOTES and it's AWESOME! Can you write about my town of Vashti, Texas?"

-Corey W., age 11, Texas

"I went to Chillermania on Saturday, April 29th, 2013. I love the store! I got the book THE UNDERGROUND UNDEAD OF UTAH and a MONSTER MOSQUITOES OF MAINE poster and a magic wand. I really want those sunglasses!"

-Justin S., age 9, Michigan

"You are the best author in the universe! I am obsessed with American and Michigan Chillers!"

-Emily N., age 10, Florida

"Last week I got into trouble for reading IDAHO ICE BEAST because I was supposed to be sleeping but I was in bed reading with a flashlight under the covers."

-Todd R., Minnesota

"At school, we had an American Chillers week, and all of the classes decorated the doors to look like an American Chillers book. Our class decorated our door to look like MISSISSIPPI MEGALODON and we won first place! We all got free American Chillers books! It was so cool!"

-Abby T., age 11, Ohio

"When school first started, I read FLORIDA FOG PHANTOMS. Then I got hooked on the series. I love your books!"

-Addison H, age 10, Indiana

"I just finished reading OKLAHOMA OUTBREAK. It was so scary that I thought there was a zombie behind me."

-Brandon C., Florida

"American Chillers books are AWESOME! I read them all the time!"

-Emilio S., age 11, Illinois

"Your books are great! Me and my friend started our own series. Your books should become a TV series. That would be cool!"

-Camerron S., age 9, Delaware

"In first grade, I read Freddie Fernortner, Fearless First Grader. Now I'm reading the American Chillers series, and I love them! My favorite is OREGON OCEANAUTS, because it has a lot of adventure and suspense."

-Megan G., age 12, Arkansas

Got something cool to say about Johnathan Rand's books? Let us know, and we might publish it right here! Send your short blurb to:

Chiller Blurbs
281 Cool Blurbs Ave.
Topinabee, MI 49791

Other books by Johnathan Rand:

#16: Catastrophe in Caseville

Johnathan Rand

An AudioCraft Publishing, Inc. book

Book storage and warehouses provided by Chillermania!©
Indian River, Michigan

Michigan Chillers #16: Catastrophe in Caseville
ISBN 13-digit: 978-1-893699-47-2

Librarians/Media Specialists:
PCIP/MARC records available **free of charge** at
www.americanchillers.com

Cover illustration by Dwayne Harris
Cover layout and design by Sue Harring

Printed in USA

CATASTROPHE
IN
CASEVILLE

VISIT CHILLERMANIA!

WORLD HEADQUARTERS FOR BOOKS BY JOHNATHAN RAND!

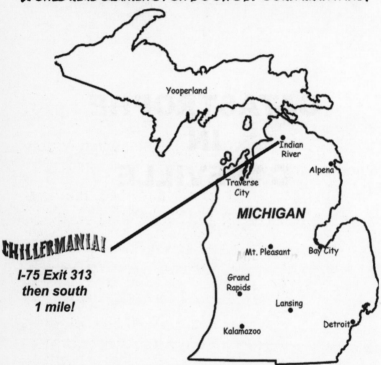

Yooperland

Indian River

Alpena

Traverse City

MICHIGAN

CHILLERMANIA!

**I-75 Exit 313
then south
1 mile!**

Mt. Pleasant

Bay City

Grand Rapids

Lansing

Detroit

Kalamazoo

Visit the HOME for books by Johnathan Rand! Featuring books, hats, shirts, bookmarks and other cool stuff not available anywhere else in the world! Plus, watch the American Chillers website for news of special events and signings at *CHILLERMANIA!* with author Johnathan Rand! Located in northern lower Michigan, on I-75! Take exit 313 . . . then south 1 mile! For more info, call (231) 238-0338. And be afraid! Be veeeery afraaaaaaiiiid . . . .

1

I awoke in darkness and knew immediately that something was wrong.

For one thing, I wasn't in my bed, that was for sure. My bed is soft and comfy; the unfamiliar bed beneath me right now felt stiff and lumpy.

Second, my cat, Munchkin, wasn't sleeping by my shoulder where he sleeps every night.

On top of that, I had a strong feeling that I wasn't in my bedroom. Even with my eyes closed, I could sense it. Something just wasn't—

Right.

I opened my eyes. Although I couldn't see

anything but inky blackness, I again felt uneasy, as if I were in strange, unfamiliar surroundings.

Where was I?

Then, as the haziness of sleep began to drift off and I became more alert, I realized where I was. As I breathed a sigh of relief, my nervousness faded.

Camping. I'm in our new camper with Mom, Dad, and my little brother, Mikey. Our neighbors are taking care of my cat while we're away. We're in Caseville, Michigan, at a campground. We came here for Cheeseburger in Caseville, the world-famous cheeseburger festival that's held every year.

I shifted and rolled to the side, careful not to bump into my brother who was sleeping in the bed next to mine. We slept in the fold-out portion of the camper, and Mom and Dad were in their bed at the other end.

I closed my eyes. A lock of my long hair fell over my face, and I reached up and pulled it away, curling it behind my ear.

Ten whole days, I thought. *Ten days of*

camping in our new camper, in a place where we'd never been before. This is going to be the best vacation ever.

We'd left our home in Toledo, Ohio, the day before, pulling our new camper that Mom and Dad had bought a couple of weeks ago. The drive wasn't too long, and I kept busy reading a book and playing video games. My brother spent the time watching a movie, while Mom and Dad took turns driving and talking about all of the fun we were going to have with our brand-new camper. We stopped at a fast food restaurant in Flint, Michigan, for lunch and made it to Caseville in the middle of the afternoon.

One thing was certain: Caseville was *a lot* different from Toledo! Toledo is a big city, and the town of Caseville is much, much smaller. Mom said that there are only several thousand people living in and around Caseville, while the Toledo area is home to over a half million!

But Caseville is really cool. It's located in Michigan's 'Thumb' area, so named because the state resembles a glove. If you hold up your right hand and look at your palm and fingers, it looks like the state of Michigan. Caseville would be located near the tip of your thumb.

Before we went to the campground, we drove around town and along the highway that follows the Lake Huron shoreline. The beaches were beautiful, and we saw lots of people enjoying the day.

But the amount of people we saw that afternoon was nothing compared to the people that would be pouring into Caseville in the coming days. The ten-day cheeseburger festival held in August attracts thousands and thousands of people every year! Dad says that people come from all across the country—and even from around the world—for the festival.

And my family would be joining the party for all ten days, eating cheeseburgers until they came out our ears, entering contests and games, and watching and listening to live music.

So, I relaxed, now that I knew where I was,

safely tucked in a small bed in our new camper at space number 18 in Caseville County Park. I closed my eyes and drifted back to sleep, without any knowledge of the horrors that were about to befall the tiny community on the shores of Lake Huron.

2

"Rise and shine, sleepy head."

The voice awoke me from a deep sleep. It was Mom. She was standing over me, smiling. Sun streamed through the camper windows. At the small dining room table opposite the tiny kitchenette, my brother sat, wolfing down a bowl of cereal.

I smiled and sat up in bed. "What time is it?" I asked.

"Time for you to get up and at 'em," Mom said with a smirk. Then, she looked at her watch.

"It's almost eight o'clock. I didn't think you'd sleep this long."

"I got up in the middle of the night and didn't know where I was," I said. "Then, I realized I was in the camper. Where's Dad?"

"He's getting our bicycles out of the truck," she said.

"Cool," I said.

Mom took a few steps and stopped at the kitchenette, and I looked around the camper. It really wasn't all that big, but it provided everything we needed: a kitchen, a bathroom with a shower, storage cabinets, and beds. Everything was much more cramped than in our house, but then again, you couldn't just put your house on a trailer and pull it behind a vehicle!

After a quick bowl of cereal, I went outside. Our three bicycles and Mikey's tricycle were parked side-by-side next to a tree. Dad was talking to a man he'd just met, and I walked over to them. When he saw me, Dad scooped his arm around me and gave me a squeeze.

"And this is my daughter, Shelby," Dad said to the man. "Shelby, this is Mr. Walker. He and his family came all the way from Kansas City, Missouri, for the cheeseburger festival."

"Hi," I said, smiling.

The man nodded. "Nice to meet you," he said. "I've got a boy about your age, with the same dark hair as yours. His is a lot shorter, though. I think he's—"

His sentence was interrupted by a distant shout.

"Dad!"

The three of us turned to see a bicycle racing toward us. The kid riding it was wearing the brightest yellow helmet I'd ever seen.

"There he is, right there," the man said.

"Dad!" the boy repeated. His bicycle raced up to us and skidded to a halt. "There's a guy juggling cheeseburgers downtown!"

"What?" his father said, chuckling. Even my dad laughed.

The boy nodded and pointed behind him,

toward town. "Honest!" he said. "It's the craziest thing you've ever seen! There's a guy in the middle of town dressed up like a clown, and he's juggling cheeseburgers!"

"How is he doing that without making a complete mess?" I asked.

"I think the cheeseburgers are in plastic sandwich bags," the boy said. "At least, that's what it looks like. But it's crazy! Wanna see?"

"Trent," Mr. Walker said, "this is Shelby McConnell. Shelby, this is my son, Trent."

I nodded in greeting, and Trent repeated the gesture.

"Wanna see?" Trent repeated, clearly directing the question to me.

I looked up at my Dad and didn't even have to ask him for permission.

"Sure," he said. "Just watch out for traffic, and don't be gone too long."

I raced inside the camper and retrieved my helmet, putting it on as I strode to my bike. Trent turned his bicycle around, and soon, we were weaving through the campground, side by side. Somewhere, someone was cooking bacon and eggs. The delicious aroma made me hungry, even though I'd just eaten a big bowl of cereal.

"He's near the center of town," Trent said as we continued through the campground. Birds chirped and darted in the trees around us.

"This I've gotta see," I said. I've seen people juggle things like knives, bowling pins, softballs, oranges, and even chainsaws. But I've never seen anyone juggling cheeseburgers.

"You won't believe it," Trent said. "And the guy is pretty good at it, too."

We left the campground and made our way through town. Although the festival wasn't scheduled to begin for another day, there were already many, many people around. Cars were parked everywhere. People filled the sidewalks and streets.

And up ahead, we saw a thick crowd gathered in a tight cluster. As we drew closer, I could see things flying in the air, arcing up and down.

"That's him," Trent said, pointing with his right arm. "That's the guy juggling the cheeseburgers."

I tried to catch a glimpse of who was doing the juggling, but there were too many people around. Some were laughing, and a few were clapping, cheering him on.

But suddenly, without warning, the laughing and clapping stopped. There was an eerie silence for a moment, and then a woman screamed. Then another. A man shouted, and then someone else screamed. Soon, downtown Caseville was in chaos, with people screaming and running in every direction!

3

"What's going on?" I said, braking to a halt. Trent did the same, and the two of us remained seated on our bicycles, looking ahead at the mayhem and madness that had enveloped the small downtown area.

"I have no idea," Trent said, shaking his head. His yellow helmet shined in the sun.

While we watched, we began to catch glimpses of different expressions. Some people were screaming, but others were laughing. Still, everyone was running away from the center of town, and in a moment, we figured out why.

I caught the movement of a small animal, a dark cat, waddling along the street.

"It's only a cat," I said.

"No, it's not!" Trent said, with a laugh. "Look again! It's a skunk!"

Sure enough, a skunk was wandering through the center of town! Everyone was fleeing in every direction imaginable, trying to get away, not wanting to get sprayed, not wanting to get covered with stinky skunk odor!

The skunk turned and went down an alleyway. People stopped running. Slowly, things began to get back to normal. Through it all, the juggler hadn't stopped his crazy juggling. He was still throwing cheeseburgers high into the air, expertly catching them before tossing them up again.

"That was funny!" Trent said. "I've never seen so many people so frightened by one small animal."

"Not just any animal," I said with a smile. "A

skunk! You'd run, too, if he was after you."

We got off our bikes and pushed them toward the center of town, closer to the juggler. The crowd was gathering once again, but people were giving wary looks over their shoulders, on the lookout for the skunk, should he return.

And one thing was for sure: Trent was absolutely right. The juggler was amazing. I counted eight cheeseburgers wrapped in plastic baggies that he was tossing into the air. He was catching them behind his back, between his legs, throwing some of them high into the air. He never dropped one.

"And this is just the festival warm-up," Trent said. "The really exciting stuff hasn't even started to happen yet."

Again, Trent was right. The exciting stuff hadn't even started. But sometimes, exciting things happen that aren't fun. Sometimes, excitement can be deadly . . . as the entire town of Caseville was about to find out.

4

One mile from downtown Caseville:

An old man sits in his dark, basement laboratory, alone. His gray hair is but a bird's nest, a tangled mesh of uneven, coarse, wiry fibers whirling and pointing in every direction. He wears thick, dark rimmed glasses, and a thick, gray mustache grows over his top lip. He is surrounded by computer monitors that connect to video cameras outside his house, so he can see if anyone approaches. His house is completely surrounded by a tall, wooden fence that hides his home and yard.

And in the yard, unseen by anyone who passes by, is a secret project . . . a project he has been working on for a long, long time.

On the wall of his laboratory are newspaper clippings of previous cheeseburger festivals from various years, announcing that year's winning cheeseburger, selected by the voting public. Some of these clippings have angry pen marks slashed through them. Others have darts stuck to them. Another clipping shows the picture of a restaurant with the caption: *Bunmaker's Cheeseburgers Goes Out of Business, Closes Doors for Good.*

Turning in his chair, he takes a sip from his coffee mug. Then, he places his fingers at a computer keypad and begins typing.

"Not long, now," he whispers as he watches the computer screen. *"The fools will finally pay. They'll be sorry they didn't choose my cheeseburger. They'll be sorry I had to close my restaurant. They'll be sorry, all right. Everyone will be sorry. This year, they'll regret not choosing Bunmaker's Cheeseburgers as the best cheeseburger restaurant in Caseville.*

They'll regret not choosing my cheeseburger as the absolute best. Yes, they'll be sorry, all right. Everyone is going to be very, very sorry."

His name is Thaddeus P. Bunmaker, and he came to Caseville years ago, hoping to get rich selling cheeseburgers, to achieve fame and fortune during the annual Cheeseburger in Caseville festival.

He did not.

His restaurant was called *Bunmaker's Cheeseburgers,* and it was located in the downtown district. However, Bunmaker could not cook well, nor could he even make a decent cheeseburger. He treated his employees and customers rudely. It didn't take long for Bunmaker to earn a bad reputation among the hardworking, kind folks of Caseville. Soon, fewer and fewer people ate at *Bunmaker's Cheeseburgers*. During the festival, his cheeseburgers did not win any contests; indeed, it was widely agreed that Mr. Bunmaker's cheeseburgers were among the worst they'd ever had.

Within only two years, people stopped visiting *Bunmaker's Cheeseburgers* altogether. Without customers, no money came through the doors. Without money, Mr. Bunmaker was forced to close his restaurant.

But as they say: *That was then. This is now.* For years, Mr. Bunmaker plotted his revenge. He vowed to get back at everyone in the village of Caseville, everyone who hadn't voted for his restaurant and his cheeseburgers. All the while, he experimented in his basement laboratory, where he spent most of his days. When he needed to go shopping, he was careful never to go into Caseville; instead, he traveled to other cities for food and other necessities, so he wouldn't be recognized.

At first, the people of Caseville thought Mr. Bunmaker had moved away. Then, they forgot about him entirely. No one around Caseville knew that while they ate, slept, laughed, and played, a madman was only a mile away, working furiously in his basement, putting together an awful, evil plan.

And now, the time has come. Thaddeus P. Bunmaker is about to unleash his revenge during the upcoming cheeseburger festival . . . and what he's going to do is unspeakable.

5

We watched the clown juggle cheeseburgers for a few minutes. Then, we hopped on our bikes and rode back to the campground. Trent told me all about his hometown of Kansas City and how he and his family lived on a farm outside of the city. He laughed a lot, and he seemed really nice. I was looking forward to spending a lot of time with him over our vacation.

And it was really cool that his family was camped right next to ours! We would get to hang out together every day.

"Wanna go for another bike ride after lunch?" Trent asked as we pulled up to our campsites.

"Sure," I said. "It'll be fun to explore the town before the big festival gets started."

In our camper, I told Mom all about Trent and the crazy clown juggling cheeseburgers. I told her about the skunk that had scared everyone away, but how everyone had a good laugh.

"That must've been something to see," Mom said.

"It was," I answered with a smile. "It was pretty funny. Where's Dad?"

"He and your brother went over to the grocery store to pick up a few things," Mom replied. She had made a bologna sandwich and handed it to me. "He shouldn't be gone too long. What are your plans for the rest of the day?"

"If it's okay, I want to go for another bike ride with Trent," I said as I took a bite of the sandwich.

"I think that's a great idea," Mom said. "It's

a nice, hot, sunny day. Be sure to fill up your water bottle and take it with you."

I finished my sandwich. Then, I went out to my bicycle and returned to the camper with my water bottle. I filled it in the sink and returned it to its holder on my bike.

Mom appeared in the door of the camper. "Don't go too far," she said. "Do you have your phone?"

"Oh!" I said as I put on my bicycle helmet. "I completely forgot."

For my birthday, Mom and Dad got me a cell phone. It wasn't very fancy, and it didn't have any games or cool things like that. It was just for making phone calls. Or specifically, for making phone calls to Mom or Dad or getting phone calls from either one of them. Still, I thought it was cool to have my very own phone, even if I didn't get to use it much.

I went back into the camper and retrieved my phone from my backpack, stuffing it into my pocket.

"See you later, Mom," I said.

"Have fun," Mom replied, "and don't forget what I told you about not going too far."

"I won't," I said, and the camper door banged shut behind me as I jogged through the campsite to my bicycle beneath a tree.

Trent was outside, too. Like me, he had filled up his water bottle and placed it in the holder on his bicycle. When I saw him, I had to laugh.

"What's so funny?" he asked.

"Your helmet," I said. "It looks like you have a fat banana on your head."

Trent laughed at this. "I think it's kind of cool," he said, "even if it does look like a big banana."

Again, we set out through the campground and into town, passing dozens and dozens of people. There was an ice cream store directly across from the campground, and a bunch of people waited in line to order tasty, cool treats. I had a little bit of money, and I thought that maybe, once we were done with our bike ride, we could stop for an ice cream cone before we went back to the campground.

We wound our way through town and over to a nearby marina. It was beautiful! There were boats all over the place and even more people. There wasn't a cloud in the sky, and sunlight glittered on the crystal blue waves. Adults and children played in the water and built sand castles on the nearby beach.

"This has got to be the most perfect place in the world," Trent said. "I mean, I like where I live, but this sure is a beautiful place."

I couldn't agree more. While I liked living in Toledo with my family and friends, Caseville sure was a great place to vacation.

We turned our bikes around and were about to start out again when Trent suddenly stopped. He cocked his head back, put his hand above his eyes to shield the sun, and stared.

"Holy cow!" he said. *"Shelby! Look at that! Are you seeing what I'm seeing?"*

I was. I was seeing exactly what he was seeing, but I couldn't believe it. Others around us had spotted the strange sight in the sky, and they, too, had stopped to stare up in wonder and disbelief.

6

High in the sky, beneath a canopy of blue, was a giant cheeseburger.

A *monstrous* cheeseburger.

It was hard to tell for sure, but it looked to be about the size of a large car or van.

"What is that thing?" someone nearby asked.

"It looks like a giant cheeseburger," someone replied. A crowd was quickly gathering, squinting up into the sky, staring at the enormous cheeseburger floating in the air.

"It's a helium balloon!" a man shouted. "It's

an advertisement for a cheeseburger restaurant. If you look close, you can see that it's tied to a string of some sort."

The man was right! It was a helium balloon that looked just like a giant cheeseburger! It was difficult to see, but a long string dangled down from it, hundreds and hundreds of feet, where it connected to something on the ground a few blocks away.

"That's so cool!" Trent said.

We continued on our bikes, and I glanced up at the sky every few moments to gaze at the giant cheeseburger. I wished my phone had a camera so I could take a picture to show Mom and Dad, but I was sure they would have a chance to see it soon enough.

We rode past the beach and back through town again. Everywhere we went, everyone was smiling and happy. People wore colorful clothing, T-shirts splashed with bright tie-dyed colors. The mood was festive and fun.

And the festival hasn't even started, I thought.

I can't wait until it kicks off.

In the meantime, my new friend Trent and I were enjoying ourselves as we explored downtown Caseville. It was fun to be out and about, on our own.

Of course, we had no way of knowing it, but we were only minutes from encountering something very strange . . . something that would lead to the most frightening experience I've ever had in my life.

7

In town, we parked our bikes, locked them to a light post, took off our helmets, and decided to walk around a little bit. Again, it was exciting to be around so many happy, fun people. Many people were going in and out of stores, buying gifts, or having lunch in restaurants. I knew that my mom said that only a couple of thousand people live in Caseville, but it was obvious that more people were arriving for the festival, seemingly by the hour. I was sure that very soon, the entire town was going to be jam-packed with people.

Trent and I went into a couple of gift shops, but we didn't buy anything. Finally, after about thirty minutes, we returned to our bikes and continued our ride.

"I hope we don't run into that skunk by accident," Trent said as we rounded a corner.

I smiled and laughed, thinking about how funny it had been earlier that morning, when the skunk appeared and scared everyone out of the middle of town.

"I think he's probably afraid to be around all these people," I said. "If I was him, I would stay far, far away."

We rode a couple of blocks until we came to the beach. Again, we parked our bikes and walked, this time through the sand down to the shore. The waves of Lake Huron were calm, and there were quite a few people taking advantage of the hot afternoon, swimming in the water and splashing around. Not far away, a mother was scolding her son for not putting on enough sun screen. To our left, someone had set up a volleyball net, and a group of teenagers were in fierce competition.

We walked back to our bikes, hopped on, and continued riding. This time, however, we took a road that led out of town, a road that wasn't filled with people and cars. In fact, after traveling only a few blocks, there were no more buildings or houses. Just forests and fields.

"Let's keep going and see what we can find," Trent suggested.

That seemed like a fine idea. We rode our bikes along the shoulder, on the gravel.

And then—

Then, we saw something that seemed a bit odd. Something out of place.

Trent noticed it first, in the distance, ahead of us. It was a wooden fence, and the planks were put together so tightly that you couldn't see on the other side. It was as if whoever built the fence didn't want to be able to see out, and they didn't want anyone to be able to see in. I had seen fences like this constructed around junk yards, and maybe that's what it was.

But I didn't think so. As we approached, we got a better look at how big the fence was. If a junkyard was on the other side, it was very small. No, this fence, although tall, confined only a small area, perhaps enough to contain one small house, nothing more.

And the *smell*.

It was faint at first, but gradually, as we pedaled on and got closer, it became stronger. There was no mistaking it.

Hamburger. It smelled like someone was grilling hamburgers. Not only that, there was also an odd, spicy scent in the air, a scent I couldn't place. Yet it was so new, so distinct, that I knew I had never smelled it before in my life. It wasn't an unappealing smell, and I wondered if someone had created some sort of special cheeseburger sauce.

"Do you smell that?" I asked.

Trent sniffed. "Yeah," he said. "It's something really spicy. Strange."

"I don't think I've ever smelled anything like it," I said.

"I wonder what's behind there," Trent said as we allowed our bikes to roll to a stop. We were on the shoulder of the road, only about twenty feet from the fence.

"Well," I said, "let's go find out. There's a small hole in the fence right there." I pointed. "That's big enough to see through. No one else is around. Come on."

We got off our bikes and laid them on the ground. We approached the fence, cautiously on the lookout to make sure no one else was around. Even before peering through the small hole, I looked around apprehensively, wondering if anyone was watching us.

I didn't see anyone, but just because no one else was around, that didn't mean we weren't being watched.

Because we were. At that very moment, someone was watching our every move.

8

Thaddeus P. Bunmaker is still sitting at his desk in his basement, working on his computer, when a motion in one of the monitors on the wall catches his attention. He glances up, then freezes.

Children.

There are two children— one boy and one girl— approaching on bicycles. While that in itself isn't all that unusual, these two children are looking curiously at the fence.

His fence.

The fence he put up so no one would be able

to see what he had in his backyard. The fence that would prevent anyone from spying on his secret project.

"And what do we have here?" he hisses under his breath. *"Two children, on their bicycles."*

He stands and leans toward the monitor for a closer look. The two children have stopped on the shoulder of the road and are now looking at the fence. They are talking to one another, but Bunmaker can't hear what they are saying.

But that doesn't matter. Mr. Bunmaker doesn't like children. Children are curious. Children are nosy. Children cause trouble.

So, when he sees the boy and the girl get off their bikes and make their way toward the fence, he is alarmed.

"Now, now, children," he says in hushed tones. *"What are you up to, children?"*

He looks toward the screen, watching the children get closer and closer to the fence. He watches them stop a few feet in front of it. Again, the two children speak to one another, but Mr.

Bunmaker still can't hear what they're saying.

But when the girl steps forward, inching her way toward the fence, leaning toward it in an attempt to peer inside, he knows he must do something. Mr. Bunmaker knows he must put a stop to this.

He spins and storms up the basement stairs, clenching his fists with every step.

"Those pesky kids are going to be sorry," he hisses. "Yes, they are going to be very sorry, indeed."

9

I was only a couple feet away from the small hole in the fence. I could see now that it was a knothole, only about the size of a quarter, but it was big enough for me to probably get a peek at whatever was inside.

I never got the chance.

Not far away, a portion of the fence—a gate—swung open, and a strange man suddenly appeared. He was the weirdest dressed person I think I've ever seen. He was wearing black pants with black shoes and a white lab coat. His hair was gray and messy, and it tossed in the wind. His glasses were so big and thick that they made him look like a beetle. He clenched and re-clenched his fists. Behind his glasses, fire burned in his eyes. There was no doubt that he was really mad.

And there was no doubt that we'd been caught spying.

"And just what do you think you're doing, young lady?" he asked. "I have video cameras all around. I was watching you." His voice was thick and raspy, like he was talking with gravel in his throat.

Both Trent and I were so shocked by his sudden appearance that we jumped back. I grabbed Trent's wrist and held tight.

The man came toward us, walking next to the fence. His eyes were wide, menacing, cruel.

"Perhaps you didn't hear me," the strange man sneered. "What are you doing here?"

"I . . . uh . . . we—"

"Yes?" he demanded.

By now he had stopped, standing only five

feet in front of us. His hands were on his hips, and his eyes bore into mine, then Trent's, then mine again. He looked like a demented grandfather, some sort of awful, mad scientist.

And I was scared like I had never been scared in my life. He was taller and bigger than me, and he'd caught me trying to peek through his fence.

Trent, trying to be brave, spoke up.

"Honest, mister," he said. "We didn't mean any harm. We just wondered what was on the other side of the fence."

"And just what did you see?" the old man pressed.

I gathered courage and spoke. "Nothing," I said, shaking my head. "I didn't get a chance to see anything."

The man eyed me warily. "Are you sure?" he asked. He spoke like a snake, and I imagined his forked tongue slithering in and out, in and out with every syllable uttered. I cringed and willed myself to look away, but I couldn't.

And just when I thought that we were really in trouble, that something really bad was about to happen, the man smiled. It wasn't a kind smile, but it wasn't a mean smile, either.

"Well," he said, "I think you children have learned your lesson. You won't come back here with your prying eyes, will you?"

Trent and I shook our heads until I thought they were going to fall off.

"No, sir," Trent said. "We're really sorry. We'll never be back again."

"Good," the man said, nodding. His smile vanished. "Because if I see you again . . . ."

He didn't finish his sentence. He didn't have to.

No more words were spoken as Trent and I hurried back to our bicycles. We got on them, turned around, and rode away, never looking back.

Finally, when we were approaching Caseville's city limits, Trent spoke.

"That dude was freaky," he said.

"He was more than freaky," I said. "He was

freaky-weird."

"What do you think is behind the fence?" Trent asked. "I mean, why is he being so secretive?"

I shook my head. "Your guess is as good as mine," I said.

"At this point," Trent said, "I don't have any guesses at all."

So, I shrugged it off. I wanted to forget about the fence, I wanted to forget about the old man. None of it was important.

Or so I *thought*.

Oh, what was behind the fence was important, all right. And the next morning, we would find out just how important it was.

Not only was it *important,* but it was *deadly*. What that old man was doing, what he had planned for Caseville and its poor residents was beyond horrifying. He wasn't merely going to cause a little trouble.

He was going to cause a *catastrophe*.

10

We stopped at the ice cream store before we went
back to the campground. After our ride, the cold,
creamy treat tasted great. Later, after dinner, Trent
and I went to the beach and went swimming. The
water was refreshing, and we had a lot of fun.

Later that night, we had a campfire. Trent
and his family, including his two older sisters,
joined us. We roasted marshmallows, told jokes,
and laughed a lot.

The next morning was a repeat of the day
before: perfect, sunny skies and warm

temperatures. Dad told me it was going to be even hotter than the day before. In short, it was going to be a perfect day to kickoff the cheeseburger festival.

I was eating a bowl of cereal with my brother when Dad came into the camper. "You guys want to go perch fishing?" he asked.

Caseville is considered the perch capital of Michigan and is known for great perch fishing.

I nodded. "I will!" I said. I liked fishing, but I wasn't very good at it, and I never caught a lot of fish. Still, it seemed like fun.

"I will, too!" my brother chimed in.

Mom shook her head. "Not me," she said. "But if you catch any fish, bring them back and I'll cook them."

"I rented a small boat and some gear," Dad explained. "We're all set to go down to the marina."

So, the three of us went fishing in a small boat. For a change, I caught a lot of fish, and so did Dad and Mike.

By the time we returned to the marina in the boat, the population of the town had surged. If I thought that a lot of people were around yesterday, it was *nothing* compared to the throngs of people who now choked the village. Cars and people were everywhere. Live music played from several locations. It was hard to believe that so many people could fit into such a small lakeside community.

Dad cleaned the perch, wrapped them up, and put them in the freezer. Mom said she would cook them later in the day and that we would have a delicious perch dinner.

I changed into a clean pair of shorts and a T-shirt and left the camper. In the next campsite over, Trent was poking at the campfire with a stick. I walked over to him.

"Hi," I said.

"Good morning," he said with a smile. "I had fun last night, around the campfire."

"Yeah," I said. "I love roasting marshmallows over the campfire. We'll have to do that again tonight."

"Man," Trent said, looking around and pointing toward town. "There are a ton of people here."

"There sure are," I replied. "You wanna go downtown and see what's going on?"

Instead of taking our bikes, we decided to walk. It was only a few blocks, so we decided that it might be easier to move in the crowds of people without the bulk of our bikes.

"Look," Trent said, pointing to the ice cream shop. "It's not even noon, and there's already a big line for ice cream."

We weaved our way through the crowds. It was like one gigantic party. Everyone was laughing and joking, and the mood was very festive. Music seemed to come from every direction. Street vendors sold T-shirts, hats, and other festival items and souvenirs.

Again, like the morning before, a huge crowd had gathered at the center of town. I didn't see any cheeseburgers flying into the air, so I figured the juggler wasn't around. The crowd must've been attracted by something else. And when we rounded a corner and got a glimpse of what was getting all the attention, I stopped. Trent stopped next to me, and both of us just stared.

In the middle of town, right in the intersection of the streets, was a giant cheeseburger. It was just as big as the helium balloon cheeseburger we'd seen in the sky the day before, but the one we were looking at now was different.

It looked *real*.

Gooey, yellow cheese dripped over the burger and onto the bun. Giant slabs of bacon formed a slick, greasy tongue. The burger even appeared to have a mouth, formed by tomatoes and pickles. And on the top bun, two ridiculously large pickles seemed to form what appeared to be eyes.

It almost looks alive, I thought. *It looks real*.

Not only that, it *smelled* real. We were still a block away, but I could already smell a delicious aroma filling my nostrils. It was almost lunchtime, so I was getting hungry. The smell of the gigantic cheeseburger made me even hungrier.

But there was another smell that I noticed, something I couldn't place.

What was it?

Dozens of people swarmed the giant burger. Many were taking pictures and videos.

"Come on," Trent said. "Let's go check it out!"

Trent started off, but I hesitated. He turned around and stopped, waiting for me.

"What's wrong, Shelby?" he said. "You look like you've seen a ghost or something."

I looked at the enormous cheeseburger that seemed to fill the entire intersection. "I don't know," I said. "I just have a really bad feeling about this."

Trent turned and looked at the cheeseburger, then turned and looked back at me.

"That?" he said. He was smiling, and his eyes were filled with excitement. "It's just a giant cheeseburger that somebody made. Come on. Let's go check it out. It's not like it's going to bite you or anything."

Once again, Trent was right. The giant cheeseburger wasn't going to bite me. What the giant cheeseburger had in store for Caseville was far worse.

11

In his dark basement laboratory, Thaddeus P. Bunmaker sits in his chair, looking up at the numerous screens mounted to the wall. In one of the monitors, there's a large crowd of people who appear to be looking back at him. No one in the crowd, of course, knows that there is a tiny video camera mounted within the giant cheeseburger, and all of them are being watched at that very moment.

"Yes, yes," Bunmaker says. He clasps his hands and gleefully rubs them together. "This is going to be perfect. Just perfect. No one suspects anything. Everyone thinks it's just part of the festival."

He continues watching as people take pictures of the cheeseburger. Some people are posing in front of the massive morsel, and others are just staring up in wonder.

"I'll show them," Bunmaker says. "I'll teach them a lesson they won't ever forget!"

He glances down at a control panel on his desk. It contains two joysticks and numerous colorful buttons. Slowly, he places his right index finger on a red button. He holds it there, while he glances back up at the screen, surveying the scene in downtown Caseville.

"All of my years of planning and work are coming together," Bunmaker says. "We'll see who will have the last laugh, this time. Just a few more minutes. All we need is a bigger crowd to gather. Then, the fun begins."

And so, he waits. He waits impatiently, with his index finger on the red button.

On the screen before him, he sees more and more people arriving downtown. They are peering in amazement and wonder at the giant cheeseburger that seems to have appeared overnight. And as a matter of fact, it had, thanks to Thaddeus P. Bunmaker.

"*Yes,*" Bunmaker whispers. "*Yes. Now it is time. Now, I get my revenge.*"

Slowly, methodically, he presses the red button.

12

"Does anyone know where this thing came from?" a woman asked.

Several people shook their heads.

"It was here early this morning, when I went to the donut shop," a man replied. "Been here ever since."

"The thing looks and smells real," another man said.

By now, the crowd had grown even more. The streets and sidewalks were packed with onlookers and gawkers. Many people were taking pictures with their phones. Others had cameras and video cameras.

"I wonder how they made it to look so real," Trent said. He pointed up at what appeared to be the mouth of the giant cheeseburger. "I mean, it really looks *real*. Look at that meat. And the cheese. Even the lettuce, tomatoes, and pickles look real."

"But lettuce, pickles, and tomatoes don't grow that big," I said. "I suppose someone could make a huge slice of cheese that big. And they probably could pack a bunch of hamburger meat into a gigantic patty. But no one in the world would be able to grow vegetables that size. Those pickle slices are bigger than trash can lids."

I sniffed the air. Now, I was hungrier than ever.

And again, I detected that odd scent that was vaguely familiar. Still, I couldn't place it.

"Let's go home for lunch," I said. "I'm starving. After we eat, we'll come back with our cameras. I want to get a picture of this thing."

"Good idea," Trent said.

We turned around. It was difficult to move through the crowd, because there were so many people. We had to zigzag around everyone. Finally, when we reached the edge of the gathering, the people thinned out, and we were able to move freely.

"I can see why this festival is so popular," Trent said. "Everyone seems to be having the time of their lives."

"And it seems like there are lots of surprises in store," I said.

Suddenly, from behind us, we heard a gasp and a muffled scream. Trent and I stopped and turned around.

The crowd didn't appear any different, except for the fact that no one seemed to be moving.

Then, to our horror, we watched someone crumple to the ground

"That dude just fell," Trent said, pointing.

We watched while another man went to the

fallen man's aid. But he, too, seemed to lose his balance. He fell forward, tumbling to the street.

The crowd was dispersing, but people were stumbling and appeared to have a difficult time walking. Other people began to fall. There were gasps and murmurs and several screams.

The carnage was about to begin.

13

Seated at his desk in his basement laboratory, Thaddeus P. Bunmaker is impressed. When the first person passes out from the sleeping gas released from the cheeseburger after he presses the button, he claps his hands with glee.

"Excellent!" he says. "Most excellent! Most excellent, indeed!"

He stands now, facing the screen, watching more and more people as they fall asleep and tumble to the ground all around the giant cheeseburger.

"Splendid," he says. "The sleeping gas is working just as planned."

While he watches, more people fall to the ground. Others are trying to help people by pulling them away or keeping them from falling down.

Mr. Bunmaker presses the button again, which shuts off the sleeping gas that is contained in a canister hidden within the cheeseburger.

He continues to watch the screen before him. Dozens of people are lifeless in the street. None are injured; they are only sleeping. The scene is chaotic. People are rushing everywhere, stepping over people, frightened and fleeing.

In the distance, away from the crowd, Mr. Bunmaker sees two people he recognizes: a boy and a girl. He recognizes them as the ones he caught yesterday, trying to peer into his yard through the fence.

"Well, well," he says. "What have we here? My curious young friends are still curious."

He watches the boy and girl, and a mischievous smirk spreads across his lips.

"Yes," he says very slowly. "Revenge is sweet."

Then, he returns to his chair. On the screen above him, people are waking up. They are getting to their knees, confused and disoriented. They don't know what's just happened to them.

Bunmaker places his hands over the control panel, and each one finds a joystick.

"And that's just for openers, folks," he says as if the people in Caseville can hear him. "What do you say we get started with the main event?"

He draws a slow breath.

"Say good-bye, Caseville," he says. "Say good-bye to your city and your infernal cheeseburger festival!"

14

"What's going on?" I asked. The scene was alarming, disturbing.

Scary, even.

Trent shook his head. "I don't know," he replied.

"Are they dying?" I asked.

Again, Trent shook his head. "I don't have any idea. But something really bad is happening."

When he said those words, my skin chilled. I broke out in goosebumps, even though the day was sunny and hot.

Gradually, some of the people who had fallen began to move. They sat up on the ground. Some of them got to their knees or were helped to their feet by someone else. It didn't look like anyone was seriously hurt, but I couldn't be sure.

"It's as if a bunch of people suddenly passed out," Trent said.

"What would cause that?" I asked.

"Sunstroke?" Trent mused.

"Maybe," I said, "but I don't think it would happen to so many people at the exact same time."

"Maybe they're just acting," Trent suggested.

"What do you mean?" I asked.

"You know, like a flash mob," Trent said. "It's when a bunch of people get together at a predetermined time and location. Sometimes, everybody just freezes in place. Some of them all begin to sing the same song."

Suddenly, I realized what he was talking about. I had seen videos of flash mobs on the Internet. Most of them were harmless, but some of them caused problems, simply because there were so many people in one area at the same time.

I shook my head. "I don't think this is a flash mob," I said. "Everyone looks too confused." I pointed. "Look at them. They're all mixed up. None of them seem to know what's just happened to them."

I heard a siren in the distance. The police were coming, or perhaps an ambulance.

"Well, it doesn't look like anyone is hurt," Trent said. "That's a good thing."

The fear that had begun to grow inside of me melted away. Whatever had happened, no one had been injured. I was sure there was a reasonable explanation for what had happened, and I was sure that, in time, we would know what it was.

I was just glad that it hadn't happened to me! If I would've suddenly fallen asleep and tumbled to the ground, I would've been freaked out, for sure!

"Let's go," Trent said. "Let's go grab some lunch and come back with our cameras. By then, there'll probably be a lot more things we can take pictures of."

We were about to turn and begin walking again, when a series of gasps caught our attention. Again, we turned back around and looked at the scene in the center of town, at the people milling about, and the giant cheeseburger in the intersection of the streets.

Not a single person was moving. They were all staring at the cheeseburger.

There was a noise. A squeaking sound. A chinking, metallic sound.

And while we watched, the enormous cheeseburger rose up, rising high on two legs, towering over the terrified spectators. Two french fries emerged from either side of the bun, forming arms. Hands made of what appeared to be hamburger were at the ends of each french fry.

It was impossible . . . but the giant cheeseburger was coming to life!

15

"What in the world—" I began to say, but I stopped short. I couldn't finish my sentence. I was too horrified.

Trent didn't seem to share my fear.

"That's *cool!*" he said.

"Cool?!?!" I said. "How can you say that's cool?!?!"

"Yeah," he said. "Somebody must've designed it especially for the festival!"

"Trent!" I said, nearly shouting. "That cheeseburger is coming alive! Don't you see?

Something is really, really wrong! First, all of those people faint and fall to the ground. Now, that cheeseburger has grown legs and arms and hands! I'm telling you, something is *not* right."

"Yeah, something's not right," Trent said. "I don't have my video camera. I'm gonna go back to the campground and get it."

He didn't seem at all bothered about what was transpiring in the center of town.

"Trent," I pleaded, "we have to get out of here. Something really bad is about to happen, I can feel it."

He turned to face me, and he looked serious.

"You're really scared, aren't you?" he said.

I nodded. "Yes," I replied. "I'm telling you, something isn't right." I pointed at the cheeseburger. "That thing isn't here as a tourist attraction. Something bad is about to happen, but I don't know what it is."

We heard another noise, and one of the cheeseburger's legs began to rise into the air. It took a slow step, placing its giant foot forward on the pavement. Then, its other leg rose up and took another step.

"Maybe you're right," Trent said. "I'm starting to get the same feeling."

The siren was getting louder and louder and was coming from behind us. We turned in time to see a police car, its lights flashing, stop on the side of the road. The siren died, and an officer in a blue uniform stepped out.

"Let's get out of here," I said. "Let's go back to the campsite."

And once again, the cheeseburger took another step. By now, there weren't too many people left in the intersection. Most had fled the scene altogether or were backed up along the sidewalks, near the storefronts.

The cheeseburger waved its arms. Its movements were jerky and robotic. It took more steps, faster this time, making its way down the street.

I had been right all along. This was no tourist attraction, created to entertain people at the festival. The cheeseburger *was* real. It really *was* alive.

And now we were about to see what the horrible thing was capable of.

16

The police officer raced past us, but we hardly even noticed him. We were too focused on watching the giant sandwich as it stormed down the street. While we looked on, the thing placed its foot on a car and stepped onto it, crushing the vehicle like a bug. Metal screeched and squawked, glass shattered and clinked as shards splintered and fell to the ground.

Everywhere, people were screaming. The police officer ordered everyone to keep back, but he really didn't have anything to worry about. No one wanted to be anywhere near the giant monstrosity that was making its way through downtown Caseville!

I realized that we were still standing in the middle of the street, that the cheeseburger was coming toward us. However, instead of fleeing and running back to our campground, Trent and I darted to the sidewalk and hid behind a parked car. That wouldn't do much good if the cheeseburger decided to destroy the car, but at least I felt safer than standing there in plain view, where we would be sitting ducks.

The police officer must've thought the cheeseburger was more than he could handle alone, because he raced past us once again and leapt into his patrol car. We could see him on the radio, behind the windshield.

"I'll bet he's calling for backup," Trent said.

"I wonder if they're going to believe him," I said. "When he radios to the police station that a giant cheeseburger is on the loose in downtown Caseville, they're probably going to make him the laughingstock of the department."

"That would be funny if it wasn't so serious," Trent said. "I had thought that someone had made the thing for the cheeseburger festival. You know, like some sort of tourist attraction."

"Maybe they did," I said. "Maybe they did, and it got out of control."

The cheeseburger stopped in the street. The top bun rose up, the bottom bun lowered, and it actually looked like the sandwich had some sort of mouth!

Then, the cheeseburger turned to the side, as if it was looking at something.

And it was.

Near the sidewalk was a little boy. He couldn't have been older than six or seven. He was just standing there, staring at the cheeseburger as the cheeseburger stared back at him. I don't know if the kid was too scared to move or maybe just fascinated by the sight of the monster standing in the street.

"I don't like the looks of this," I said. "I don't

like the looks of this at all."

Then, the unthinkable happened: the cheeseburger raised one leg high into the air and held it.

The little kid wasn't going to have a chance.

17

By sheer instinct, Trent and I sprang. I knew it was crazy to even *think* we could reach the boy in time, but we couldn't just stand there and watch it happen. Somehow, it would make things even worse if we didn't at least try to save him.

So, we ran as fast as we could, not even thinking about what could happen to us. The only thing I could think about was the possibility, however remote, that we might—*might*—be able to save the boy.

"*Run!*" I shouted to the kid, but by now, he

was too terrified. He screamed, but he didn't move.

Trent reached him first. He dove, wrapping his arms around the boy, tucking and rolling as the two hit the pavement just as the cheeseburger's leg came down. I dove to the side and rolled out of the way, narrowly missing being stomped.

By now, Trent was on his feet, carrying the little kid in his arms as he fled to a safer distance. Somewhere, a woman shrieked.

"Jackson! Jackson! Oh, my gosh, Jackson! Are you all right?"

Then, I saw her. She had been sitting on a curb not far away. I wondered if she had perhaps fainted like many of the other people. She was disoriented and confused, dazed and sleepy, but it was obvious that she was the boy's mother.

Meanwhile, the cheeseburger continued to move farther down the block. I had gotten out of its way just in time, and now I was back on my feet, running down the street. I leapt onto the sidewalk, continued running, and met up with Trent at the end of the block. He had let go of the kid, who raced back to the arms of his grateful mother. He was crying as she scooped him into her arms. Then, she carried him into one of the stores.

"This is getting way out of hand," Trent said, as we paused to catch our breath at the street corner.

"It got way out of hand five minutes ago," I said. "This whole thing is absolutely crazy!"

For the most part, the street was now deserted. Most people had fled, taking off in their cars, running back to the campground, or ducking into the many stores that lined the streets. We could see dozens of people peering out glass windows, staring in horror as the cheeseburger continued down the block.

"At least it's heading away from us," Trent said.

He spoke too soon. At that moment, as if the cheeseburger heard us speaking, it stopped. It spun, and now we were facing it. We were almost a full block away, so I didn't feel threatened, but I was ready to take off running at a moments notice if I needed to.

It was strange, but the cheeseburger actually seemed to be studying us. It was looking at us as if it had never seen a human before, as if it had traveled to a different planet and discovered some sort of strange new life form.

Trent also noticed this. *"It's like it's studying us,"* he whispered.

Then, the giant cheeseburger began to move. This time, however, instead of coming toward us or going the other way, it walked to the side of the street. Using its french fry arm and its burger hand, we watched as it pulled a stop sign from the ground! It held the sign in its hand like a giant, red lollipop.

"What's it going to do with that?" I asked.

"Probably eat it," Trent said.

But that's not what the cheeseburger did. Instead, it raised the sign over its head, holding the sign like a spear. Without any warning at all, the giant cheeseburger launched the stop sign at us!

Quickly, I darted to the side, rolling onto the

sidewalk and crawling to the entryway of a store. I was safe.

Trent, on the other hand, wasn't going to be so lucky.

18

In the laboratory, Thaddeus P. Bunmaker laughs. It's an evil, wicked laugh. He sits at the controls, both hands on the joysticks, watching the screens on the wall. He delights in the mayhem and madness he's creating in downtown Caseville.

"They laughed at me then," he says. "Look who's doing the laughing now." Again, he laughs.

On the screen, the cheeseburger is causing enormous chaos and destruction in the street. It has squished a car, and it scared a little boy half to death. Oh, Bunmaker wasn't going to hurt the child, which is why he made the cheeseburger hold its leg in the air until the very last moment, until the other boy had snapped up the little child and pulled him out of harm's way. Then, in a show of power, Bunmaker used the controls to bring the cheeseburger's foot forcefully down onto the pavement.

His revenge has been years in the making. The cheeseburger, of course, isn't a real cheeseburger at all. Bunmaker has carefully designed and built a remote-controlled, battery-powered robot. Internally, the cheeseburger contains a mass of electronics and computer gadgetry. Externally, the cheeseburger is made of mostly plastic materials, fiberglass, and foam. He's spent hundreds and hundreds of hours to make it look exactly the way it does: like a colossal cheeseburger, a supersized, sinister sandwich, complete with deadly accessories to torment an unsuspecting community.

And now he's unleashed it upon Caseville.

"It's those same two kids who were snooping

around here yesterday," he says to himself as he glances at the screen and sees the boy and the girl at the end of the street. "Let's have a little more fun with them, shall we?"

Working at the controls, he moves the cheeseburger toward the curb. With his left hand, Bunmaker taps some computer keys. His right hand controls the joystick, which controls the french fry arm and burger hand of the cheeseburger. The cheeseburger reaches out, pulls a stop sign from the ground, draws it back above the top bun. Bunmaker takes aim at the two children and lets the stop sign fly through the air toward his two targets. He can see that the girl is already getting out of the way, diving to the sidewalk.

But the boy? The boy isn't going to be quick enough, and the stop sign is going to make a direct hit.

19

Crouched down in the doorway of the store, I could only watch as Trent turned, flailed his arm, and tried to get out of the way.

He couldn't. He wasn't fast enough.

The sharp end of the stop sign—the part that had been buried in the ground—hit Trent squarely in the chest.

It went right through his body.

I screamed and covered my eyes. I have never been able to handle the sight of blood, and I was certain that I was about to see a lot of it.

Trent yowled. I forced myself to open my eyes, expecting the worst.

Trent was standing on the sidewalk, with the sign protruding from his chest. He was sideways to me, and I could see that the sharp end of the sign went through his body, and the post was sticking out nearly two feet through his back.

But Trent didn't seem to be bothered by this at all. Instead, he simply raised his right arm, and the stop sign clanged to the street.

I couldn't believe my eyes! I was certain the sign had pierced his body, but it hadn't. Instead, it went between his arm and his ribs, making it appear that he'd been struck in the chest. He hadn't, and he was unhurt. It was a miracle.

"Oh, my gosh!" I shouted. "Trent! I thought you got speared by that sign!"

Trent was shaken. His eyes were wide, and he was trembling.

"I thought I did, too!" Trent said. "If I would've moved the other way just a couple of inches, I would be dead!"

"We've got to get somewhere safe," I said. "Come on. Let's go inside the store."

Trent glanced through the windows of the store; then, he looked at the cheeseburger at the end of the block.

"No," he said. "I want to go back to the campground. I'm sure my parents are worried about me. Your parents are probably worried about you, too. I'm sure that they must have heard what's going on. They might be looking for us right now."

I thought about this. Trent had a good point. If Mom and Dad knew what was going on, if they knew the danger I was in, they would be worried sick.

But they haven't come looking for us, I thought. Then again, not much time had gone by. Maybe they didn't know yet.

Right or wrong, I decided Trent's idea was better. Sure, we might be safer if we went into a store, but we might be trapped there, as well. Plus, the cheeseburger didn't seem like it could move very fast, and I felt we could easily outrun it.

"Okay," I said. "Let's circle around to the next block and try to stay away from that thing."

I stood and joined Trent by the curb. We looked up the street.

The massive cheeseburger was no longer paying attention to us. It was slowly ambling down the middle of the road, heading the other way. On both sides of the street, frightened people cowered next to stores. I could see the shadows of people huddled in their cars. They were horrified.

We ran in the opposite direction, circling around the block until we reached the next street. Then, we turned. If my calculations were correct, we would have only a couple of blocks to go before we would arrive at the entrance to the campground.

Here, the streets were a flurry of activity. People were running everywhere, getting into their cars and speeding off. Some were shouting, calling out to friends or family members. Some were crying. Others were on their phones in frantic conversation. It was a confusing, chaotic scene.

We ran up the street, but before we even reached the intersection, we knew we were in trouble. For whatever reason, the cheeseburger had also turned a corner. Now, it approached the intersection and stopped. Once again, it stared right at us, and I had a creepy feeling that it somehow knew who we were. It was almost as if it was hunting us.

We stopped.

The cheeseburger stared at us.

"Well," Trent said softly. His voice trembled. "We can backtrack and go back around to the other block. It might not follow us."

"But what if it does?" I asked.

"I guess we'll have to figure that out if it happens," Trent replied.

As it turned out, we wouldn't get the chance to find out if the cheeseburger was following us. But we *were* about to find out that the thing had a few deadly tricks under its bun.

20

Thaddeus P. Bunmaker is a happy man. In fact, he's happier now than he has been in years. Probably happier than he has been in his entire life. Not only is his giant cheeseburger robot performing just as planned, his act of revenge is playing out even better than he'd expected. He experiences sheer joy as he watches the helpless people flee in terror. He can hear their shrieks and cries, and he is elated.

"Thaddeus P. Bunmaker," he says, "you are a genius. You are simply a genius!"

He is relaxed, comfortable. Seated in his basement laboratory at the controls, watching the carnage unfold on the screens before him, he is calm and self-assured. He knows he is unstoppable. Now that he has unleashed his giant cheeseburger, now that his plan for vengeance is unfolding, he feels powerful and strong.

He carefully controls the cheeseburger as it makes its way through the center of town. Just for fun, he stomps on several more cars and a motorcycle. They are destroyed instantly.

The cheeseburger reaches the end of the block and turns the corner. By now, Bunmaker has forgotten all about the two nosy children. He had watched in dismay as the stop sign missed the boy. It had been close, but his aim was off by mere inches. No matter. Those two children didn't factor into his plans. If they got away, they got away. To Bunmaker, it wasn't any big deal.

No, Bunmaker had bigger plans.

But when he reaches yet another intersection and sees the boy and girl at the end of the block, he has yet another diabolical idea.

"Might as well show those children and others in the area how hot a summer day can get in Caseville," he says quietly.

For a moment, he watches the children watching him. Then, he places his thumb on a button at the top of the left joystick. He turns the cheeseburger, and a nearby van comes into view in the screen on the wall.

"Now, there's a splendid object," he says with a grin. "I wonder how the residents of Caseville like their vehicles: charred, grilled, deep-fried, or well done?"

He presses the button.

21

"Look," Trent said. "It's up to something."

The cheeseburger hadn't moved in several seconds, but now his mouth—if that's what you could call it—was opening. The hamburger patty seemed to lower, and toppings of pickles, tomatoes, and lettuce shifted upward.

What's it doing? I wondered.

While we watched, the cheeseburger turned and appeared to look down at a nearby van. Then, the massive thing reared back a little and leaned forward. Suddenly, a huge plume of fire sprayed from its mouth, completely engulfing the parked van!

"Holy smokes!" Trent shouted. *"It just lit that van on fire!"*

Once again, the weight of the situation was heavy on my shoulders. This wasn't fun and games; this was Serious Business. Now, more than ever, I knew that we had to get out of the downtown area. We had to get somewhere safe, before the two of us were grilled like a hamburger and went up in smoke like the van.

The cheeseburger triumphantly raised its french fry arms and pumped its hamburger fists into the air. Then, it charged down the street, once again heading in our direction.

Without a word, Trent and I spun on our heels and ran to Prospect Street, which was the first street we came to.

"That way!" I shouted, as our sneakers pounded the hot pavement. "That street should take us toward the campground!"

We turned left onto Prospect Street. I

managed a glance over my shoulder and saw the cheeseburger. It was still coming after us, but it was turning from side to side, emitting plumes of flame. Trees ignited, and even several buildings were now on fire.

And while I knew that it would be only a matter of minutes before more police and firemen arrived on the scene, that wasn't going to help us at the moment. Right now, there was no stopping the cheeseburger. If we wanted to live, we were going to have to save ourselves.

We continued running along the street. In yards and driveways, people were rushing to get to their homes. Several people leapt into their cars and sped off. One car was nearly crushed by the cheeseburger, but the driver swerved just in time and raced away.

But there was something else that we hadn't considered.

We weren't familiar with the streets of Caseville. While I was sure that Prospect Street headed in the general direction of the campground, there was something about the street we couldn't have known . . . until it was too late.

Trent suddenly slowed and pointed.

"Oh, no!" he said.

I looked at the sign he was pointing at. It was big and yellow and rectangular. It read:

DEAD END.

Prospect was a dead end street.

And behind us, the monstrous cheeseburger kept coming.

We'd reached a dead end, all right . . . in more ways than one.

22

Thinking quickly, I came up with an idea.

"Let's cut through the yards!" I said. "If we can cut through the yards, maybe we can make it back over to Main Street! We can follow it back to the campground!"

"But what do we do then?" Trent asked. "If that thing keeps following us, it's going to follow us all the way to the campground!

"Let's think about it on the way," I said. "We can't stay here. That thing is still coming!"

We cut through somebody's yard, past the

side of the house, through another backyard, and through yet another yard. Just as I suspected, we reached Main Street, right near the bridge that crossed over a river.

Seeing the water gave me an idea.

"Trent!" I shouted as we ran. "If we make it to the campground, we can make it to Lake Huron. If we can do that, we can go into the water. I don't think that thing will follow us into the water!"

"Great idea!" he said. "We can warn our families, and they'll probably come with us! "

We continued along Main Street. By now, when I turned around, I couldn't see the cheeseburger. But when I heard a crash behind us, I shot a quick glance over my shoulder. The cheeseburger had done the same thing we had: he'd cut through the yards. He was still breathing flames and lighting things on fire. I could see black and gray smoke rising up above the city.

But thankfully, all of a sudden, we heard a siren. And another. Then another.

"Finally!" Trent said. "More help is on the

way!"

Ahead of us, a police car, its lights flashing and sirens blaring, came squealing around the corner. We darted to the side to stay out of its way and it sped past, so fast that I could barely make out the two uniformed officers in the front seat. The vehicle screeched to a stop on the bridge, not far from the rampaging cheeseburger.

That was a terrible mistake.

The cheeseburger, having no fear, stormed up to the police car. In an unexpected move, the behemoth thing jumped into the air and came crashing down onto the vehicle in an explosion of metal and glass!

I stifled a scream by covering my mouth with both hands. Trent gasped.

The police car was nearly flattened. The two officers never had a chance to get out.

23

The incident seemed to freeze both of us. We felt horrible for the policemen, but there was nothing we could do.

Meanwhile, the cheeseburger moved away. It stepped aside, staring at the demolished police car, clearly proud of its handiwork.

And then, miraculously, we saw something move in the wreckage.

"Look at that!" Trent said, pointing. "One of the cops is still alive!"

"The other one is, too!" I said. "He's crawling

out from the other side of the car!"

One of the police officers stood. He was carrying a shotgun, and he leveled it at the cheeseburger. A sharp blast rang out, then another. And another.

The shotgun had no effect on the cheeseburger. We could see a couple of small pieces flying off of it, but the blasts did nothing to stop the thing. The other officer began firing his handgun at the cheeseburger, with the same effect. No matter how many times they fired, it didn't seem to do anything to the cheeseburger.

Although we were some distance away, we could hear one of the police officers shouting into his radio, calling for backup.

"They're going to need more than just police backup!" Trent said. "They're going to need the Army, the National Guard, and the Marines!"

"And the Air Force, Navy, and Coast Guard, too!" I said.

Now that we were a safe distance away, we didn't feel the need to flee to the campground. I knew that the situation was still very dangerous, but I was also curious and fascinated by the scene that was unfolding. I guess that's why so many people stop to see traffic accidents and other exciting scenes. Some things are simply incredible and unbelievable, and they just seem to command your attention. Some scenes are just impossible to pull your eyes away from.

Like the one we were watching. Trent and I just stood there on the shoulder of the road, watching as the two police officers tried to stop the monster cheeseburger, firing away with their weapons.

Finally, the officers stopped shooting and ran to the parking lot of a church, realizing that their tiny weapons were useless against such a massive beast. There was no way they were going to be able to tackle this problem alone. The best thing they could do was wait for help to arrive.

"Those cops are lucky that cheeseburger hasn't spit fire at them," I said. "He's been burning up things all over town."

"Maybe that's why they moved back," Trent said. "Just to be safe."

But the cheeseburger had no intention of using fire. Once again, it opened its mouth . . . only this time, an enormous barrel emerged, pointed directly at the two police officers.

The cheeseburger had a cannon!

24

In his basement laboratory, Mr. Bunmaker laughs. As he watches the van go up in flames, he can hardly contain his delight.

"Oh, this is getting good," he says, watching the two children run down the street. Controlling the cheeseburger, he makes the monster sandwich follow them. Along the way, the cheeseburger emits dragon tongues of fire, igniting trees and buildings.

"Yes, now the real fun is beginning," Bunmaker says. "This is more fun than a barrel of monkeys!"

Using the joysticks to control the cheeseburger, Bunmaker makes the giant sandwich follow the children as they turn left onto Prospect Street. In the computer monitors on the wall, he can see people fleeing into their homes and cars.

"Yes, yes," he says. "It's all your fault, people. You wouldn't know a good cheeseburger if your life depended on it. And now, my friends, your life truly *does* depend on it."

He presses the button on the joystick, releasing yet another plume of fire from the cheeseburger. This blast completely engulfs a spruce tree in a nearby yard. Through the computer monitor, Bunmaker can see the horrified people inside the house, watching helplessly as the tree goes up in flames.

Suddenly, he hears a police siren and watches as the squad car comes squealing around the corner, lights blazing, headed toward him.

"Splendid!" Bunmaker says. "I love surprises. Now, the police are in for a little surprise of their own!"

After he causes the cheeseburger to leap into the air and crush the police vehicle, Bunmaker moves the sandwich back into the street. The policemen begin firing at the cheeseburger; however, in the computer screen in front of him, it appears that the blasts are aimed directly at Bunmaker.

"Fire away, boys, fire away," Bunmaker says. "Your weapons won't stop me. Nothing you can do will stop me."

When the policemen stop firing, they flee into a church parking lot where they take cover behind a parked vehicle.

"Not so fast," the old man says. "I still have a surprise for you."

On the control panel at his desk is a square, red button. He presses it once. This causes a cannon barrel to extend out from the cheeseburger. The red button begins flashing.

In the computer screen on the wall, he can see the horrified looks of the police officers as they peer out from around the parked vehicle. They are talking among themselves, and Bunmaker can't hear what they're saying.

Then, the two policemen begin running across the parking lot.

"Oh, not so fast, gentlemen," Bunmaker hisses. Again, he laughs. "Not only are we going to have a little more fun, we are going to have an absolute *BLAST!*"

Aiming the cannon barrel carefully, he presses the flashing red button.

25

When the policemen began to run across the parking lot, I realized they'd made another terrible mistake. Perhaps they thought they'd be able to outrun the cheeseburger or dodge any cannon fire, but I knew that they'd underestimated the giant sandwich. In their attempt to flee, they were now fully exposed, with no protection, nothing to hide behind.

"They were lucky once," Trent said, "when that thing crushed their car. But I don't think they're going to be so lucky this time."

As much as I hoped Trent was wrong, I knew that wasn't going to be the case. I was sure it was going to be the end for the two policemen.

They were halfway across the parking lot when a solid red beam shot out from the cannon. At first I thought it was an arrow of some sort, but it wasn't.

It was a *liquid*.

The gooey, red fluid hit the police officers with so much force that it knocked them off their feet. They were completely covered in bright red goop. They had gone from blue to red in less than one second.

"Wait a second!" Trent said. "Do you know what that is?"

I shook my head. "Some poison of some sort?"

"Ketchup!" Trent said. "That thing just blasted those two cops with ketchup!"

We watched as the cheeseburger turned, aimed the cannon barrel into the air, and let out another blast. This time, ketchup hit the church, covering the entire front and the roof, dripping from the eaves and onto the parking lot.

"This is going to be one big mess to clean up," I said.

"I don't think we need to worry about the mess," Trent said. "I think we need to worry about staying alive."

"Yeah, you're right," I said. "We'd better—"

I stopped speaking in mid-sentence. A breeze had licked across my face, bringing with it the smells of the cheeseburger. I could smell the ketchup, mustard, relish, and the meat.

But I could also smell something else, something that was familiar. I couldn't place it—at first.

Then, it suddenly came to me, and I knew that I had solved a big part of the mystery.

26

"*Trent!*" I blurted. *"Do you smell that?"*

"Smell what?" he replied. "You mean the cheeseburger?"

"Yes, that," I said. "But that *other* smell! That's the same scent we smelled yesterday, when we were at that mean old man's house! Remember? When we got close to the fence, we could smell something that was strange. I'm smelling that again, right now!"

Trent sniffed the air. "Yeah, you're right," he said.

"That mean old man has something to do with this," I said. "That's why he was being so secretive. That's why he was so mean to us. I'll bet we were close to finding out something he didn't want us to know about."

"The cheeseburger?" Trent asked.

"Exactly!" I answered. "He's got to be behind this! He was acting awfully suspicious yesterday."

"But what can *we* do about it?" Trent asked.

"We don't have to do *anything*," I replied. "But we can let the police know. We can tell them what we suspect."

"And just what do we suspect?" Trent asked.

"That the old man has something to do with the cheeseburger," I said. "Maybe he created it. Maybe he's inside of it, right now, controlling it."

"That's crazy!" Trent said.

"Do you have a better explanation?" I asked. "I'm telling you: that old man has something to do with this mess, and we need to call the cops and let them know."

"Did you bring your phone?" Trent asked.

I shook my head. "I forgot it in our camper."

"Then, let's go back to the campground," Trent said. "Our parents are probably worried about us, anyway. We can tell them what we know, and then call the police."

It wasn't difficult to find our way back to the campground, where we found a flurry of activity. Terrified people were rushing here and there, packing up tents, campers, and all of their belongings. There was a big line of vehicles exiting the campground. Everyone was leaving Caseville in fear for their lives.

And behind us, smoke continued to rise into the air above the city. It was total madness.

But when we reached our campsites, we didn't find our parents. My brother and Trent's sisters were gone, too.

I bolted into our camper, looking for Mom or Dad or Mikey. They weren't there.

In the campsite next to ours, Trent shouted. "My parents are gone!"

I found my phone and left the camper and

went outside, frantically looking around.

"They're probably out looking for us," I said. "They're probably worried sick."

"Now what?" Trent asked.

I touched Mom's speed dial number that was programed into my phone.

"I'm calling my mom," I said.

The call wouldn't go through. Instead, I got a message telling me that due to heavy usage by other customers, service had been interrupted. The message told me to try my call again later. Instantly, I disconnected and tried Mom's number again. I got the same message.

I spotted my bike beneath the tree.

"Now what?" Trent asked again.

"We go on our own," I said.

Trent's brow furrowed as he looked at me.

"What do you mean?" he asked.

"We take our bikes and go back to that man's house," I said.

"You're crazy, Shelby!" Trent said.

I shook my head. "We might find something

there that will help us figure this whole thing out."

"What if the old dude is there?"

"We won't know unless we go out there. Come on."

Trent shook his head, but I continued to argue with him.

"We've got to do *something*," I said. "If we can stop that thing—that cheeseburger—from destroying the entire city, we've got to do it."

"I say we wait here," Trent said. "Our parents will come back to see if we're here."

"We might not have the time," I insisted. "*Caseville* might not have the time."

Finally, he gave in.

"All right, all right, I'll go," he said, raising his hands in defeat. "But I think we're making a big mistake."

We hopped onto our bikes and slipped our helmets on.

"We're probably safer over at the old man's house, away from the downtown area," I said. "Here, in the city, that savage sandwich might be capable of anything. The farther we get from Caseville, the safer we'll be."

At least, that's what I hoped. And as we rode out of the campground, weaving in and out of the line of bumper-to-bumper vehicles, I kept telling myself that we were doing the right thing, that we were going to be okay, that everything was going to work out fine.

Still, I kept wondering what we'd discover at the old man's house, what we would find. Would we figure out this whole thing?

The answers we were about to get were more unbelievable—and more shocking—than I could have ever imagined in a million years.

27

There is no happier man in Caseville.

For years, Thaddeus P. Bunmaker has been preparing for this day, the day he would terrorize the innocent residents of Caseville. Now, his misguided attempt at unwarranted revenge is spreading mayhem and madness all across the small city in Michigan's Thumb.

When he unleashes a torrent of ketchup upon the two police officers, he is so excited that he spills his coffee. He doesn't bother cleaning it up. He is too focused on watching the two officers stumbling around, covered in slimy, red goo. In fact, he is so focused on the destruction the cheeseburger is causing downtown that he doesn't even look at the other screens on the wall.

"A direct hit!" Bunmaker says, clapping his hands. "A perfect shot!"

For the time being, he is happy to simply watch as the policemen struggle to get to their feet. Soon, they stumble off and vanish behind the church.

"This is so much fun!" Bunmaker says. "Let's see . . . who shall I terrorize next?"

He moves the joystick, which causes the giant cheeseburger to turn. As it does, the view in one of the computer screens changes, and now he can see a tree and a building on fire.

"Yes, yes," he says as a new idea comes to him. "I'll destroy every cheeseburger restaurant in Caseville!"

Suddenly, he sees something rushing toward him. It's a large, red vehicle. As it approaches, he recognizes the fire truck.

"Now, what have we here?" he says. "Just what do you fellows have up your sleeve?"

Several men wearing gray coats and yellow helmets leap from the long, red vehicle and begin unrolling hoses.

Bunmaker looks alarmed. This is something he's overlooked, something he hasn't planned on.

"No, no, no," he says in serious, hushed tones. *"We can't have this. If my creation gets wet, all of the electronics will short circuit. I cannot let this happen."*

While the firemen continue to unravel hoses, Bunmaker reaches for another button. This one is round and green. He presses it once; it begins to blink. A display on the control panel lights up. It reads: *Cannon 2 deployed.*

The firemen see that another long cannon is emerging from the mouth of the cheeseburger, and they quicken their already frantic pace.

"Too late, friends," Bunmaker says. He presses the green button and watches with glee as a waterfall of green, chunky relish is heaped upon the firemen and their fire truck. It is so thick and sticky that the men can barely move. Bunmaker presses the button again, and yet another green, gooey blast covers the men.

"Ha!" Bunmaker proclaims. "Thought you'd stop me with a little water, eh? Well, I beat you boys to the punch. I'm just going to sit here and *relish* in my victory!"

He laughs at his own bad pun and continues to watch the struggling firemen.

"Sorry to leave you in such a sticky situation, men," he says, "but I've got some cheeseburger restaurants to destroy."

Using the joysticks, he moves the giant cheeseburger away from the fire truck.

But he's distracted by a sound.

He pauses at the controls, listening. It's a heavy, constant, thumping sound.

Wompwompwompwompwomp . . . .

Then, he realizes what it is.

"So," he says as he makes an adjustment to the controls. The view in the screen changes, showing blue sky as the cheeseburger's head is tilted back.

A blue and white helicopter comes into view.

"Ah-ha!" Bunmaker says. "Just as I suspected. How shall we deal with this new threat?"

He looks at the control panel, then back at the helicopter on the screen.

"Ketchup? Relish?" he says. "Mustard?" Then, he shakes his head. "No, no, those won't do," he says. He smiles and places his finger on a button. "I think I'll order one flame-broiled helicopter, medium rare," he sneers . . . and presses the button.

28

We couldn't risk going straight through the downtown area, so we took some side streets until we wound up on the road that led to the old man's house. We heard more sirens. In the distance, we heard a helicopter approaching.

I glanced over my shoulder to see the blue and white helicopter make a wide turn above the city. Then, as it was descending, an enormous tornado of fire rose up beneath it! The chopper veered dangerously to the side to miss the orange and yellow flames, and for a minute, I thought it was going to roll over. Instead, it recovered and quickly rose higher into the air to a safer distance.

"Did you see that?!?!" I said to Trent.

"Yeah," Trent said. "This just gets crazier and crazier by the minute."

Soon, we saw the large wood fence appear farther up the road. As we approached the old man's house, fear began to well up inside me. It felt like there was a rock in my stomach, churning and knocking around. I was nervous and scared. Now that we'd actually reached the old man's home, I wasn't so sure if it was a good idea, after all.

But I pushed away my fears, telling myself that all we were going to do was look around. I doubted that we'd actually be able to do anything to *stop* the old man, if he was even responsible for what was going on. But if he *was* responsible, and there was something we *could* do to stop him, we'd have to try.

"Are you ready for this?" I asked.

"As ready as I'm ever going to be," Trent

said. "What are we going to do?"

"First of all, let's see if the old guy is even home," I said. "I'll bet he's not. I'll bet he's inside that cheeseburger, controlling it."

We snuck around the side of the fence, surprised to find a large section open, exposing a short, paved driveway . . . and a small home with white vinyl siding. All of the windows had curtains, and all of them were closed. We couldn't see in, but that also meant that whoever was inside probably couldn't see out. And there were several signs posted on the fence and the house that read: *NO TRESPASSING*.

"Now what?" Trent asked.

"We just go up and knock on the door," I said, very matter-of-factly. At least, it *sounded* matter-of-fact. Inside, I was terrified. I didn't want to knock on the door. I did not want to even *be* here. But I knew that this was our chance. This was our chance to find out some answers. I knew that the old man was somehow involved with what was going on . . . all we needed to do was prove it.

Slowly, we walked up the driveway, tiptoed up the porch, and inched our way to the front door. I raised my fist and was just about to knock, when I noticed something.

Something about the front door.

It wasn't closed all the way.

Then, we heard laughter.

Somewhere in the house, the old man was laughing.

"I don't think we should be doing this," Trent said quietly.

It was then that I also changed my mind. We shouldn't be here. Yes, it had been my idea to come to the old man's house. But now that we were here, standing at his front door, I realized that it probably wasn't the best idea, after all.

"You're right," I agreed. "We should probably just go back and tell the police and let them deal with it."

And that's what we probably would have done, had we not heard the old man talking in a loud voice. From somewhere within the house, we heard a chilling sentence.

"It won't be long now!" he said. "It won't be long now, and the entire city of Caseville, along with its cheesy cheeseburger festival, will be completely destroyed!"

Hearing that, I changed my mind again. I knew we had to stop him. Somehow, whatever he was doing, whatever he was up to, Trent and I had to do whatever we could to save Caseville.

Gathering up all of my courage and taking a deep breath, I placed the palm of my hand on the front door.

Slowly, I pushed it open.

We were going inside.

29

I was very, very nervous as we walked into the old man's home. I knew we were doing something we shouldn't be doing, but I really didn't feel like we had any other choice. Whatever he was up to, he was destroying the city of Caseville. If there was something we could do to stop him, we had to do it, even if it meant going into the old man's house uninvited.

And right away, as we looked around the living room, we knew something really strange was going on.

The walls of the living room were covered with newspaper clippings and articles. They were all articles with pictures about the cheeseburger festival. Some of them had big, angry black slash marks through them, as if someone wanted to destroy the article. Others had darts stuck to them.

"This is really weird," Trent whispered.

"No kidding," I whispered back. *"This guy is some sort of lunatic."*

We heard more laughter come from somewhere in the house, but we couldn't be sure where it was coming from.

Tiptoeing cautiously, we made our way through the living room and into the kitchen. Here, more articles were posted on the walls and on the refrigerator door. They all had something to do with the cheeseburger festival, most of them announcing a particular restaurant or person as the winner of Caseville's finest cheeseburger. And the kitchen was messy, too. There was ketchup, mustard, relish, blobs of cheese, and pieces of meat all over the counter, the cupboards, the sink, and the walls.

"Let's keep looking for him," I said quietly.

"What are we going to do when we find him?" Trent whispered back.

I shrugged. *"Who knows? But we've got to stop him. You saw what he almost did to that helicopter. Somehow, he must be controlling the cheeseburger. If we can stop him, we can stop the cheeseburger. We can stop Caseville from being destroyed."*

Then, we heard the old man speak again, but I couldn't tell what he was saying. His voice sounded like it was coming from the other end of the hallway.

I pointed. *"Let's go,"* I whispered.

We made our way through the kitchen and into the hall, where we tiptoed softly on the carpeting. We heard laughter again, closer this time, and we knew we were headed in the right direction.

Finally, we came to an open door with steps that led down into a basement.

"He's down there," I whispered to Trent. *"We have to go down there."*

Trent looked at me. Clearly, he didn't want to do this. I didn't, either, but like I said: we really didn't have any choice. As much as I didn't want to do this, I think any kid in our position would do the same thing. Nobody wants to see innocent residents of a small town suffer.

Slowly—very slowly—I raised my left foot and placed it down onto the first step. Then, my right foot followed. Trent did the same. Ever so slowly, we took the stairs, step by slow step, down into the basement. The good thing was that the stairs were lined with a wall on either side, which meant we couldn't be seen. However, it also meant that we couldn't see the old man. We would need to walk all the way down the stairs and peer around a doorway, hoping we wouldn't be spotted.

The old man spoke, suddenly and quickly, and it surprised me.

"There!" he said excitedly. "Now I'm finally ready! Caseville is about to be wiped off the map, and there's not a single thing *anyone* can do about it!"

The time had come. We didn't have time to think, we didn't have time to wonder what to do. We simply had to *act*. What we would do, we had no idea. We didn't know what we were getting ourselves into.

But we had to act, and we had to act *now*. Without worrying about the noise we would make, without wondering what we were about to find, Trent and I bounded down the last half dozen steps, into the basement, ready to challenge the old man.

Ready to fight for the survival of Caseville.

30

At the bottom of the stairs, Trent and I received the shock of our lives.

We weren't looking at a basement as much as we were looking at a laboratory. Shelves lined the walls. They were filled with electronic gadgetry, glass beakers, and all sorts of odds and ends, and I had no idea what all this stuff would be used for. The only light came from a single, bare bulb in the middle of the room and from a half dozen flat screen monitors mounted on a wall. And beneath the monitors, with his back to us, was the old man. He was sitting in a chair, staring up at the screens before him. His fists were on the table, and he was clutching a joystick in each hand.

"He hasn't heard us!" Trent whispered into my ear. *"He didn't hear us come down the stairs!"*

The old man was so focused on what he was doing that he didn't even know we were there. His back was to us, and the only thing he was paying attention to were the screens above him, mounted to the wall.

And by watching the monitors ourselves, it was easy to understand what was going on. The man was controlling the cheeseburger. Seated alone, here in his basement, he was controlling the cheeseburger's every move. He and he alone was responsible for causing the destruction and chaos that was now erupting in Caseville.

"We've got to stop him!" I whispered. *"We've got to get him away from that control panel on his desk."*

"Let's see if we can grab him and pull him away," Trent whispered. *"Maybe if we smash the*

control panel, it will stop the cheeseburger."

I couldn't come up with any better idea, so I agreed with Trent.

"Okay," I said. "*When I count to three, we'll rush him. As soon as we're able to pull him back from the desk, one of us will have to grab the controls. Break the handles, smash something, do anything. Just try to damage it, so he can't work it anymore. Ready?*"

Trent nodded.

"Okay," I whispered. "*One . . . two . . .*

—three!"

Ready or not, we charged the old man. Yes, the idea was crazy, but we knew we had to stop him.

Would we succeed?

That question was about to be answered.

31

When we charged, the man heard us and spun in his chair. His huge eyes were bulging beneath his thick glasses, and his mouth hung open. Clearly, he was not only surprised, but quite shocked at the sight of two kids charging him.

"You!" he shouted. *"You kids—"*

Trent grabbed one arm, and I grabbed the other.

"What are you doing?!?!" the old man cried. "What do you think—"

But we pulled him out of his chair and away

from the desk and the control panel before he could finish speaking. We were smaller than he was, of course, but he wasn't very strong and didn't have fast reflexes. Trent and I were able to wrestle him to the floor without too much difficulty. When he tried to get up, Trent fell on top of him to try to keep him down.

I used the opportunity to reach for the control panel. Bouncing to my feet, I looked at the array of switches and dials on the desk, at the two joysticks and the numerous, colored buttons.

"You let me up this minute!" the old man wailed. "You let me up, or I'll—"

He grunted and groaned as he tried to get up, but Trent held fast, using every last ounce of energy and strength to keep the old man on the floor, to keep him from reaching the control panel.

"Do something, Shelby!" Trent shouted.

"Don't touch anything!" the old man wailed.

Frantically, my eyes scanned the control panel, darting over all of the buttons and levers, trying to figure out what to do. I thought that I could just smash it, which was our original plan. But now I had another thought.

If I smash the control panel, that might make the cheeseburger go out of control completely. I might make things worse than they already are.

Then, I saw a large, black button on the side.

"*Shelby!*" Trent shouted. His voice was pained as he continued to struggle with the old man.

I stared at the black button. Block letters beneath it read:

WARNING! EMERGENCY SELF-DESTRUCT.

I glanced up at the screens. Some of them showed scenes of fires burning around town and in trees and buildings on fire. Police officers and firefighters were everywhere, trying to contain the blazes.

"*Shelby!*" Trent shouted again, louder this time. "*Do something!*"

"There's an emergency self-destruct button here," I said.

"*Don't press that!*" the man wailed. He was

even more agitated than before. *"Whatever you do, don't press that!"*

I lowered my hand and placed my index finger on the button.

Trent shouted again, even louder.

"Shelby! Do something! *Do something!*"

I pressed the button . . . and all of the screens on the wall suddenly went blank.

32

The old man started screaming. Trent was still managing to hold him down, but I knew he wouldn't be able to for much longer.

"You vile children!" the old man shouted. "You don't know what you've done! You don't know what you've done!"

"What did you do?" Trent asked as he continued to struggle with the man.

"I pressed the emergency self-destruct button," I replied.

"You've ruined everything!" the old man

wailed. "You children have ruined everything!"

Trent couldn't hold the man any longer, and he was thrown to the side. The old man got to his knees, but we weren't going to wait for him to get to his feet.

"*Run!*" I shouted, and we sprang for the stairs, taking them two at a time, never looking back to see if the old man was following us. We raced down the hall, through the living room, out the front door, and to our bicycles by the fence. I didn't even take the time to put my helmet on. I just left it on the ground, and Trent left his, too. We jumped onto our bikes and began pedaling like mad. We didn't talk, we didn't stop until we were far away from the old man's house.

We could hear sirens still screaming, and they grew louder and louder as we got closer to the city. Angry smoke billowed into the sky, although it wasn't as thick and full as it was earlier.

"What do you think happened?" Trent asked as we rode up to the outskirts of town.

"I'm not sure," I replied, "but I would imagine that something happened to the cheeseburger when I pressed that button."

"Why do you think that old man was doing that?" Trent asked. "I mean . . . why would someone want to ruin the cheeseburger festival?"

I shook my head and stopped pedaling, allowing my bike to coast along the pavement.

"I don't know," I replied. "But in looking at some of the newspaper articles he had taped up around his house, it looked like he was mad about something. Did you see the way he had scratched out many of the articles and pictures? It was almost as if he was jealous of the festival or jealous of those who had won some of the contests during the cheeseburger festival."

"Still," Trent said, "that's no reason to do what he did."

"People do crazy things, sometimes," I said.

We rounded a corner, getting our first glimpse of the downtown area. What we saw was worse than we could have ever possibly imagined.

33

Most of the sirens had stopped shrieking, but a bunch of police cars and fire engines lined the streets, their lights whirling and flashing. Several firefighters were hosing down a building that was still smoking. Police officers rushed about, crisscrossing the street.

And everything—even all the people—were covered in colorful goop! Ketchup, mustard, relish, and blobs of cheese were splashed everywhere, covering cars, trees, buildings, even people! The air smelled of burned cheeseburgers.

Trent and I said nothing as we pedaled

downtown. We were stopped by a policeman who held up his hands.

"Sorry," he said. "Can't let you go any farther. Not until this mess gets cleaned up."

"But we know who did it!" Trent blurted.

The policeman looked at Trent, then at me. His eyes widened.

"What?" he asked. "Who?"

"An old guy not far from town," I said, pointing behind us. "He was controlling the cheeseburger from his basement!"

The policeman looked at us suspiciously, as if he didn't believe me.

"How do you know this?" he asked warily.

"We were just there," Trent said. "We just stopped him. We pulled him away from the control panel, and Shelby pressed a button that caused the cheeseburger to self-destruct."

"Boy, did it ever," the policeman said. "That thing blew up and sent pieces of gooey stuff all over the city."

"Really?" I asked.

The policeman waved his hands. "Just look around," he said. "This place is a mess. But at least that thing isn't on the loose anymore. It's not causing any more destruction. But tell me again how you became involved in this."

So, we spent the next hour explaining everything to the policeman and another policeman who joined him. We told them all about how we had discovered the man's house the day before, how we only wanted to see through the fence to see what was on the other side when the old man caught us. I told them about the strange smell I had detected at his house and how I had picked up that same scent just a little while ago, when the cheeseburger was creating so much havoc.

"That's why we went to his house," I said. "We knew the old man had something to do with what was going on. And if he did, we knew we had to try to stop him before he destroyed Caseville and ruined the festival."

"Well," one of the policemen said. "I don't

think the festival is ruined. But there sure is a big mess to clean up."

The policeman sent a couple of other officers to the old man's house to investigate. Meanwhile, around town, word quickly spread among the residents that Trent and I had been responsible for stopping the man and his robotic cheeseburger. People that we didn't even know came up to congratulate us and shake our hands, thanking us for saving Caseville and the cheeseburger festival. And as Trent and I both suspected, our parents had been frantically looking for us. They found us while we were talking to the policeman, and we had to tell them the entire story all over again.

"We were really worried," my mom said to me.

Trent's parents nodded. "We were worried about both of you," Trent's father said. "But we're glad you're both okay."

"We're fine," I said, "but I'm starving. I haven't eaten a thing since breakfast."

Mom and Dad laughed. "Well," Dad said, "I

guess we'd better feed our heroes."

Trent and his family joined us, and we walked around town to look for a restaurant that hadn't been damaged by the cheeseburger or by the explosion, a place that was still open and serving food. But we stopped when we saw a crowd gathered on the sidewalk near a store. Glass was shattered, and glittering pieces were littered all over the pavement.

But among the pieces of glass, we saw something horrifying. Up until that point, we'd thought that no one had been hurt. Somehow, everyone in Caseville had escaped with their lives, with only a few people suffering very minor injuries.

Now, we realized that wasn't the case.

On the sidewalk, face down, was the body of a woman. Her clothing was torn, she was covered in blood . . . and it was obvious that she wasn't alive.

34

I took a deep breath.

What had happened? I wondered. *Was the woman killed when the cheeseburger blew up?* If so, that would make *me* responsible for her death.

It was an awful thought, and I felt horrible.

But the people around the dead woman were smiling and laughing, and I couldn't figure out why.

Then, two men picked up the woman and carried her off. Her body was stiff as a board, and I sighed and laughed.

It was only a store mannequin! Somehow, the window had been blown out, probably from the exploding cheeseburger. A store mannequin had been knocked out of the window, and she was covered in ketchup!

"I thought that was a real woman!" Mom exclaimed.

Trent's mother laughed. "Me, too!" she agreed.

We found a restaurant that was open. We all had cheeseburgers, and they were delicious. While we ate, strangers came over to talk to Trent and me. We had to tell our story several times. Everyone seemed interested in what had happened and what we had done. Lots of people shook our hands and thanked us.

"You guys are celebrities in this town," Trent's dad said.

"I don't feel any different," I replied. "I'm just glad I'm not starving anymore."

Everyone laughed, and I remembered the saying: *All's well that ends well.*

Except, of course, for the old man. We learned later, from the news, that the man's name was Thaddeus P. Bunmaker. We found out that he'd come to Caseville years ago with dreams of opening a cheeseburger restaurant and winning all kinds of awards. But that didn't happen, and he became angry and jealous. He spent years making a giant, robotic cheeseburger that he could control remotely from the laboratory in his basement. His plan was to destroy Caseville and ruin the cheeseburger festival.

And I also solved the mystery about the strange smell, the scent that had enabled me to put two and two together, linking the old man to the cheeseburger. The scent actually came from an acid in the plastic cheese to make it look drippy and real. That's what I'd smelled when we first happened upon the man's house. It occurred to me then that if I'd been able to peer through the knothole in the fence, I probably would've spotted the cheeseburger in the backyard, where Mr. Bunmaker had built it.

So, it didn't end all that well for him. He was arrested, and now he faced years and years in jail.

And Caseville's cheeseburger festival wasn't canceled or postponed. Everyone in the city pitched in, helping clean up the streets, the cars, the buildings, even the trees. It didn't take very long with the help of so many people. Soon, the city was pretty much back to normal. A few windows had been boarded up, but they would be repaired soon.

And I had a blast! It was the best vacation I'd ever had, and I was thrilled to hear Mom and Dad making plans to come to next year's festival.

The only sad thing was that when the festival was over, it was time to go home . . . and that meant I had to say good-bye to Trent. We'd hung out together a lot over the week and had become great friends. I would miss him. Sure, we could stay in touch by calling or emailing. But I had gotten used to meeting him after breakfast and hanging out all day.

It was late morning, on our last day. Although it was cloudy, it was still a very hot day. Trent's family was busy packing up, and my family was, too. There wasn't much for me to do, and Trent had already packed up his belongings and put them in their vehicle.

"Want to go grab an ice cream cone?" he asked.

"That would be great," I replied, and the two of us walked through the campground to the ice cream shop on the other side of the street. We sat on a bench eating our ice cream and talking about how much fun we'd had during the week.

While we were talking and eating, a boy about our age recognized us.

"Hey," he said as he approached. "You guys are the ones who stopped that giant cheeseburger."

I nodded, and Trent spoke. "Yeah," he said.

"I'm Quinn," said the boy.

"I'm Shelby," I replied, "and this is Trent."

"You guys are heroes," the boy said.

"Oh, it was no big deal," I said.

He wanted to know what had happened, so, once again, Trent and I related everything that we'd gone through, how we'd discovered the old man, how we'd been chased by the cheeseburger, and how we had returned to the old man's house to stop him from destroying the town.

"That's bizarre," the kid said when we'd finally finished. "But it's not quite as bizarre as what happened to me in Grand Haven, where I live."

"Where's that?" I asked.

"Grand Haven is on the other side of the state," he explained. "On Lake Michigan."

"What happened there?" Trent asked.

"I don't know if I should tell you," he replied. "It's pretty scary. People freak out when I tell them what happened."

I looked at him curiously. "What happened?" I asked. "What was so scary?"

So, he bought an ice cream cone, sat down on the bench across from us, and told us all about the ghostly haunting of Grand Haven.

And let me tell you . . . he was absolutely right. What happened to him was probably one of the scariest things I'd ever heard.

Next:

Johnathan Rand's

MICHIGAN
CHILLERS.

#17: A Ghostly Haunting in Grand Haven

Continue on for a FREE preview!

"Quinn, can you give me a hand for a minute?"

I rolled my eyes, closed my book, and put it on my bed. Whenever Dad asks me to help him out 'for a minute,' it's usually something that takes hours.

"Be right there," I called out, and I sat up and got off my bed.

And I was just getting to a good part, I thought, glancing down at my book. *Guess it'll have to wait.*

I left my bedroom and walked down the hall

to the living room. Dad was kneeling in front of a gigantic contraption, a large, box-like piece of equipment with all sorts of switches, dials, blinking lights, meters, and a computer screen that was dark. Of course, this was nothing new. Dad was always working on electronic gadgetry, equipment that he designed and built himself.

Now, I'm sure lots of adults build electronic equipment as a hobby. But my dad is a little different. My dad is a ghost hunter. During the week, he works as a salesman at a car dealership. However, on the weekends, evenings, and almost every spare moment, he spends his time investigating haunted houses.

My friends think this is kind of cool, but in reality, I think my dad is a little nutty. I don't say that to be mean or disrespectful; I think even my dad himself knows he's a bit different. After all: how many parents will pick up their son at school and take them to what is reported to be a haunted house? My dad has done this with me dozens of times.

At first, I thought it was kind of fun. A few years ago, Dad was watching a ghost hunting show on television. He was completely fascinated, and by the time the show was over, he'd decided he wanted to be a ghost hunter, too. He read all sorts of books, watched all sorts of movies, and built his own equipment to try to detect ghosts. I went with him a bunch of times, but we never found any evidence of a real haunting.

Still, my dad wasn't deterred. Once in a while, he would capture something on video, something that moved or didn't seem right, and he would claim that it was proof that it was a ghost. I didn't think so. I never saw anything—not a single thing— that lead me to believe ghosts were real.

That was all about to change on a cold, snowy day in my own hometown of Grand Haven, Michigan.

2

Just as I suspected, I wound up helping out Dad for a few hours. Something wasn't working right on the machine he had been building, and I wound up handing him different tools while he tinkered away at the machine. Finally, later in the day, he got it working.

"There," he said as he stood up. "Now, I'll be able to record variations of temperature to a digital file. The temperature variations will be converted to a visible picture, and will be able to actually see the changes."

"Cool," I said, but I really wasn't all that interested. I went back to my bedroom and read for a while, then put on my snowsuit, boots, hats, and gloves, and went outside. It was snowing lightly, and across the street, Angela Parker was trying to build a snowman. Angela is my age—12—and I've known her all my life.

When she saw me, she stopped what she was doing and waved with a gloved hand. I crossed the street.

"Trying to build a snowman?" I asked.

"It's not going very good," she said with a defeated shrug. "It's too cold, and the snow isn't packy."

"We're supposed to get a snowstorm tomorrow," I said. "It's supposed to get a little warmer, and we're supposed to get a lot of heavy, wet snow."

"That will be perfect for building snowmen," Angela said.

"And for having snowball fights," I said.

Angela abandoned her attempts at making a snowman. Instead, we gathered up our sleds and hiked to a nearby hill. Although the conditions weren't very good for making snowmen, they were perfect for sledding. The snow was fast, and we spent the rest of the day speeding down the hill, flying over bumps and tumbling off our sleds when we took a bad turn.

Later, when it started getting dark, we went to my house. Mom had just got home from work, and she offered to make us hot chocolate. Dad was still in the living room, fumbling around with his gigantic electrical contraption.

"Is your dad still obsessed with hunting for ghosts?" Angela asked me quietly as she glanced at my dad in the living room.

I nodded. "He's bound and determined that he's going to find proof that ghosts exist."

"Maybe they do," Angela said.

"My dad is convinced that they're real," I said, "but in all the times I've ever been with him,

I've never seen any proof. He seems to think that sudden changes in temperature prove that ghosts exist. Or, he'll see something that he thought moved on its own and think that a ghost was responsible. But he's never been able to catch anything like that on camera."

"What's that thing he's working on the living room?" asked Angela.

"Some newfangled machine he built. He claims that he'll actually be able to *see* changes in temperature when they happen. He says so be able to make a video that will record the changes and convert them to images. He says that will be proof that a house really is haunted."

Angela sipped her hot chocolate. "If he actually can prove that ghosts exist," she said, "you guys will be rich."

"That would be nice," I said, "but I don't think it's going to happen."

Oh, it was going to happen, all right. Only, Dad wouldn't be the one making the discovery. It was going to be Angela and me. For the first time in my life, I would have absolute, horrifying proof that ghosts were real, that haunted houses really *do* exist.

And it was all going to happen the very next day, in an old home on Lake Michigan, on the outskirts of Grand Haven.

3

The next day was Sunday. Dad made eggs and bacon as he always does on Sunday mornings. My older brother, Alex, slept in and missed breakfast. So, it was just Mom, Dad and me sitting around the table.

"A big snowstorm is supposed to move in later today," Mom said.

"Cool," I said. "I hope we get so much snow that we don't have any school tomorrow."

"I'm going to need your help again today," Dad said, and he popped a piece of bacon into his mouth. "There's a house over on North Shore Drive, on Lake Michigan. Tony isn't going to be able to make it today, and I'm going to need some help with my equipment."

Tony Simms is a friend of my dad's. They often hunt ghosts together. Sometimes, I think Mr. Simms is nuttier than my dad.

I really didn't want to help, but I didn't see any way to get out of it. Besides: it probably wouldn't take too long.

"Do I have to stay?" I asked.

Dad shook his head. "It'll only be for a couple of hours, and all I need is for you to help me load the gear into the house. There's a big hill in front of it, and you can bring your sled if you want."

That sounded fun. While it would be kind of boring to hang out inside the house while my dad fiddled around with equipment, it would be a blast to find a new sledding hill.

"Can Angela come?" I asked.

Dad shrugged. "Sure, if she wants to."

I called Angela after breakfast and asked if she wanted to go along.

"Is it a haunted house?" she asked.

"My dad probably thinks so, or else he wouldn't be hauling all of his equipment over there."

"Sure, I'll go," Angela replied. "That sounds like a lot of fun."

"Good," I said. "Come on over any time."

Angela knocked on the door about ten minutes later, wearing her red winter coat, black snow pants, black boots, a red hat, and red mittens. We helped Dad break down all of his equipment in his garage workshop and load it into the back of his van. Then, we climbed inside and were on our way.

The sky was gray and it was snowing lightly. An inch of new snow covered the ground. Again, I found myself hoping that there wouldn't be school the next day. That would mean an extra day of sledding and playing outside.

It was only going to take us twenty minutes to get to the house. While he drove, Dad told us a little bit about it.

"A retired couple recently bought the house and moved in," he explained. "Soon after, strange things started happening. Things started moving on their own, and the man and woman started hearing weird noises and even voices. One night, they even saw a ghostly figure walking down the stairs. It scared them so much that they decided to move to a hotel while they figured out what to do. They haven't returned to the house since."

"So they called you?" I asked.

"Yep," Dad replied with a nod. "They want to find out for sure if the place really is haunted."

"Then what are they going to do?" Angela asked.

"I don't know," said Dad. "I don't get rid of ghosts, I just find them."

I looked at Angela, and she grinned and rolled her eyes. I knew she was thinking the same thing I was: Dad had never found any proof that ghosts existed.

We turned right onto North Shore Drive and headed north. After going about a half-mile, Dad slowed the van.

"There's the driveway, up ahead."

Dad turned left, and we went down a winding driveway lined with snow on each side. By now, the snow was really coming down. Big, fluffy flakes the size of cotton balls created a curtain of white in front of the van. It was snowing so hard that it was difficult to see much of the driveway.

"Looks like you might get your wish," Dad said.

"What's that?" I asked.

"If it keeps snowing like this," Dad said, "you're not going to have school tomorrow."

"I hope so," I said.

"Me, too," said Angela. "We haven't had a snow day in a long time."

The snow was falling so hard that it obscured the view of the house. We didn't see it until we were right in front of it, and let me tell you: I got a sudden chill that had nothing to do with the cold weather or the snow.

But it was Angela who suddenly gasped and pointed.

"Oh my gosh!" she said. "Look at that!"

At first, I didn't see anything.

"What?" I asked. "What is it?"

"Right there!" Angela said excitedly. "Standing next to that tree!"

I strained my eyes to see through the falling snow.

"I see it!" Dad said.

Finally, I could make out the dark figure. It was a white tailed deer! Which, of course, wasn't all that uncommon. We often saw deer near our home, and all over Michigan. However, we were really close to her. In fact, I don't think I'd ever been so close to a deer before.

Quick as a flash, the deer bounded off into the nearby woods, where she vanished.

"That was cool!" Angela said. "She was really close."

Then, our attention returned to the house. Through the thick haze of heavy falling snow, we could make out its features. It was three stories tall with lots of windows. A couple of rooms on the upper floors had sliding glass doors with balconies. I assumed they must be bedrooms or rooms for entertaining.

And it was Angela who said the exact same thing I had been thinking.

"This place is creepy," she said. "Who on earth would want to live in a place like this?"

"Actually," Dad said, "there's a lot of history behind his house. It was built in the 1920s, and was owned by some famous movie star. Not sure who. But there have been reports of the house being haunted going all the way back to the time it was built."

While I didn't believe in ghosts, I had to admit that if there ever was such a thing as a haunted house, I was looking at it. Angela was right: it definitely was creepy-looking.

"Well, let's go have a look," Dad said. "Then, we'll load all of my gear inside."

Angela and I slipped out the passenger side door, and Dad exited the drivers side. The three of us walked through the falling snow to the house, where we stopped at the front porch. Dad dug a single key from his jacket pocket.

"Here we go," he said, and he stepped onto the porch, slipped the key into the lock, and pushed the front door open. "Don't forget to knock the snow off your boots."

Dad stepped into the house, and Angela and I followed.

We were in a large foyer. There was a coat rack with several coats hanging on it. A few pairs of shoes and boots were placed next to the wall, and there was a closet with the door hanging open. It was filled with various winter coats.

Dad continued walking, and we followed him down a hallway lined with colorful paintings. To our left was a kitchen, and to our right was an enormous living room with a huge fireplace made of stone. It was filled with furniture, and there were many pictures and paintings on the walls. There was an empty coffee mug on a small table in front of the couch. A book was upside down and open on the armrest of a lounge chair. A pair of slippers were placed next to the fireplace.

"It looks like they just got up and left everything," Angela said.

"I think that's what they did," Dad said. "The man told me that he and his wife were so frightened that they didn't take time to pack anything more than a suitcase full of clothing. They wanted out of the house, and fast."

Now that I was in the house, I didn't have that creepy feeling that I had before. Outside, when I was looking at it through the falling snow, there was something strange, something unnerving about the home. Inside, it didn't appear to be anything more than it was: an old home built a long time ago.

Dad walked into the kitchen. When he was out of hearing range, I turned to Angela and smiled.

"See any ghosts?"

Angela shook her head and smiled. "Not a single one," she replied. "I'm more interested in finding that sledding hill."

On the far side of the living room was a big picture window that faced Lake Michigan. We walked to it, but it was snowing so hard that the only thing we could see was a wall of white.

"That hill could be right there," I said tapping the glass. "But it's snowing so hard, that we would never be able to see it."

Dad called out from the kitchen. "Okay guys," he said, "let's get that stuff hauled in so I can get started."

He was already in the hallway, and Angela and I followed him back into the foyer. That was where we found something very strange.

Strange . . . but not scary or horrifying.

No, the scary, horrifying things were to come later. But what we were about to discover in the foyer should have given us a warning that someone—or some*thing*—was in the house besides us.

ABOUT THE AUTHOR

Johnathan Rand has been called 'one of the most prolific authors of the century.' He has authored more than 75 books since the year 2000, with well over 4 million copies in print. His series include the incredibly popular **AMERICAN CHILLERS, MICHIGAN CHILLERS, FREDDIE FERNORTNER, FEARLESS FIRST GRADER,** and **THE ADVENTURE CLUB.** He's also co-authored a novel for teens (with Christopher Knight) entitled **PANDEMIA.** When not traveling, Rand lives in northern Michigan with his wife and three dogs. He is also the only author in the world to have a store that sells only his works: **CHILLERMANIA!** is located in Indian River, Michigan and is open year round. Johnathan Rand is not always at the store, but he has been known to drop by frequently. Find out more at:

www.americanchillers.com

Johnathan Rand travels internationally for school visits and book signings! For booking information, call:

1 (231) 238-0338!

All AudioCraft books are proudly printed, bound, and manufactured in the United States of America, utilizing American resources, labor, and materials.

USA